# SHADOWS OF THE SHIFTERS

### BELLA FROST

# ACKNOWLEDGMENTS

Thanks to:

Creative Cover Book Designs for the cover and formatting.

https://www.facebook.com/groups/
CreativeCoverBookDesigns

*For the ones that supported me through the years of writing these books.*

*To my dearly loved Boxer dogs my children that have crossed the Rainbow Bridge. You have left paw prints on our hearts forever.*

*To my family, Louise and Marty who read through and guided me with the books. My husband Kyle and Father in law John.*

*Thanks for letting me use you as my characters and your property to harbor all my shape shifters.*

*Thanks to the neighbors in Kentucky that told the stories that helped inspire some of the book.*

# TRIGGER WARNING

# CONTENTS

# 1

## "THE MEETING"

Just as Victor was setting down the coffee pot after pouring himself a cup, he heard footsteps coming down the hallway. He turned to see his colleague, Sarah, entering the kitchen with a yawn.

"Morning, Victor," Sarah mumbled, rubbing her eyes sleepily. "You're here early."

Victor grinned and gestured towards the coffee and pastries. "Thought I'd treat everyone today. Help yourself."

Sarah's eyes lit up at the sight of the breakfast spread. "You're a lifesaver, Victor. I forgot my breakfast this morning."

The phone rang again in the office. Victor glanced at Sarah before heading back to his desk to answer it. Little did they know that this call would be the start of a chain of events that would change their lives forever.

"Hello, this is Victor Donovan. How may I assist you? Yes, the property is still available. The family is willing to accept a cash price. Financing is not an option, that is perfectly acceptable, sir. I can meet you there in approximately 45 minutes. Do you have the address? You do? Wonderful, then I'll see you at the front gate in 45 minutes. Goodbye, Mr. Smith."

As Victor hung up the phone with Mr. Smith, Sara approached him with a curious look on her face. "What's the verdict? Is he serious about the Saxon property?" she inquired, eager for some good news. Victor flashed a smile and nodded.

"Yes, he seems genuinely interested. I'm meeting him at the property later today." Sara clapped her hands in excitement,

"That's fantastic news! It's been on the market for so long, I was starting to lose hope." Victor chuckled, understanding her sentiment. The Saxon property had been a tough sell – a sprawling estate with a rich history.

Victor arrived at the property and found Mr. Smith waiting for him.

"Hello, Mr. Smith, I'm Victor Donovan. It's a pleasure to meet you."

"Hello, Victor, nice to meet you too."

"How much do you know about the property?" Victor asked.

"I know it's 117 acres and there are no buildings or utilities on the land. I believe the asking price is $150,000?"

"That's correct, Mr. Smith. There used to be two homes on the property. The first one was built in 1839 by the Stellar family. Then in the late 1890s, the Saxon family bought the property, and it has been passed down through their family for over a century. Martha Saxon was the last person to live here - she was born here and gave birth to all of her children on this land."

"What happened to her home?" Mr. Smith asked.

"When Martha got older, she fell down the stairs and was unable to get help for nearly two days as she lived alone. I was a close friend of hers and would often help with farm work and cleaning around the house, but I didn't visit every day. When she was found, she was badly injured and had to be airlifted to a hospital before being sent to a nursing home where she eventually passed away. Her children donated the house to the Historical Society who carefully dismantled each board and reassembled it in town as a historical display. They also took most of her furniture, which was over a hundred years old. She lived completely off the grid with no phone, electricity, or running water." Victor exclaimed.

"That is truly incredible. It's a shame they had to sell the house. I would have loved to keep it in its original condition and location on the property." John says.

Victor drives Mr. Smith down the long driveway, over the creek, and up the logging path. The area is filled with hickory trees, black walnut trees, and wild plants growing everywhere. As the land is rolling, the trail goes through Beaver Creek and back up a hill. Half a mile in, it splits off into two paths - one leads all the way around the woods to Sulfur Mountain, while the other takes you to an open field. Victor brings Mr. Smith to the highest point of the field and they get out of the truck to take in the view of trees surrounding them.

"It's beautiful," says Mr. Smith as they start walking towards where Martha Saxon's house used to be. Victor points out a path by a large black walnut tree that leads to old Stellar foundation and a creek for fishing and swimming.

"There are even caves to explore on this property," he adds.

They get back in the truck and head towards the gate.

"I'm ready to put down $5,000 as a deposit. Draw up papers for a cash offer of $125,000 for the place as is," states John Smith to Victor.

"But sir, the Saxon family won't accept anything less than $150,000 for this property."

"How do you know for sure? It's cash money without any financing involved." Mr. Smith responds with certainty,

"I know the Saxon family and they won't do it. They've already lowered the price from $200,000 to $150,000 over the years because there have been no offers." Victor insists,

"Well then they should be happy with my offer. Make it to them." However, Victor shakes his head and says, "I'm sorry, Mr. Smith, I can't do that."

"Looks like I'll have to find someone else to do business with," Smith said firmly, shaking Victor's hand before turning to leave.

He was not satisfied with Victor's uncooperative attitude and had no intention of giving up on this opportunity.

Victor remained quiet as Mr. Smith walked away. The truth is, Victor didn't care if he sold the property or not. It rightfully belonged to him, but somehow the Saxon family managed to get a lawyer who convinced his aunt Martha to remove him from her will and forbid him from attending her funeral. The Saxons and Victor had always been at odds; they accused him of manipulating Martha into including his name in her will. In fact, Martha's daughter Ida even went so far as to claim that Victor had caused her mother's fall down the stairs and left her there without calling for help, all so he could inherit the property. However, when Victor found Martha still alive two days later, he had no choice but to call for help. Unfortunately, the fall had resulted in a stroke that left Martha paralyzed on one side and with difficulty speaking. With no way to tell her side of the story, Victor was cleared of any wrongdoing.

Meanwhile, Mr. Smith was furious with how Victor Donovan refused to entertain any offers from the Saxon family for the property. As a real estate agent, it was unethical for him to behave in such a manner. His job was to present any potential offers to the seller and let them decide whether or not to accept them. As he drove back towards his hotel, he passed by Country Real Estate office and decided it was worth a shot. He made a quick U-turn and parked at their lot before walking into the office.

"Hi there, can I help you?" greeted a friendly woman behind the front desk.

"Yes ma'am, I just saw a property with another agent who refused to take my offer to the owners," Mr. Smith explained his situation.

"Please, come into my office," Debra said, gesturing towards the door. "My name is Debra Jones, and I am the real estate broker." As they walked into her office, she asked, "And what is your name?"

"I'm John Smith," he replied.

John proceeded to tell Debra about his interest in the Saxon property and his offer of $125,000 with a deposit of $5,000. Debra reassured him that there shouldn't be any issues and that she would present his offer to the owners immediately.

"I'll make sure to get things moving as quickly as possible," Debra promised.

"Thank you, Ms. Jones. I'll give you a call in a couple of days to check on the progress," John said gratefully before leaving the office.

A few weeks pass and John receives a phone call from Debra Jones to come sign papers for the closing on the property.

# 2

## "THE DISCOVERY"

JOHN SMITH's voice echoes through the trees as he drives his
Kawasaki Mule up the dirt-logging road to the top of Sulfur
Mountain. He narrowly avoids hitting his dog, Hurley, and
scolds him for running in front of the vehicle. The road is
surrounded by tall, barren trees and rolling hills dotted with
rocks and fallen trees that will need to be cleared. As he
surveys the area, John takes note of all the repairs that need to
be done fixing fences, replacing poles, and securing barbed
wire and hog wire. On his way back down through the pasture,
John spots Hurley hiding behind a massive black walnut tree
that has been standing for over 100 years. His attention is
drawn to an old rope hanging from one of its branches -
possibly an old swing. After calling for Hurley, John continues
down towards the creek and can hear the sound of a waterfall
as he approaches. There, he finds Hurley playing in the water.

John's thoughts wander as he takes in the natural beauty of the trees around him. The hill opposite him is massive, with a wall of rock on either side lined with trees reaching for sunlight. He follows the edge and sees clay with tree roots exposed below. The creek flows slowly, its water crystal clear and teeming with fish. John can't help but think about bringing his fishing pole here for some fly fishing. As he walks along, he notices the beavers' handiwork: timbered trees and chewed stumps with deep teeth marks. He wonders if the tree tasted bad or if it was too big for them to tackle. His attention then turns to an old fireplace and the foundation of a house nearby. John imagines how it must have looked back in 1839 when it was first built by the Stellar family.

The foundation of the house is raised about 18 inches off the ground and forms a perfect square. The only visible remnants of the doors are in this small area. With each step, John imagines what it would have been like to live in this house: the smell of fresh flowers from the pasture, homemade food cooking on the wood burning stove, and the sound of children playing in the nearby creek. As he turns around, he sees that part of the fireplace still stands, made from granite found in the creek bed.

"This must have been built in the early to mid-1800s," John thinks as he strokes his chin.

He begins to search the floor of the old foundation, hoping to find something amidst the layers of dirt. After a few minutes, he notices a shiny object and bends down to pick it up. His surprise quickly turns to shock as he realizes it's a ring with part of a human finger still attached.

"How did this get here?" John wonders aloud.

His mind races with questions - should he call the sheriff? Take it to their office? Or keep quiet?

As he ponders his options, John notices Hurley standing across the creek, eerily still. He cautiously makes his way over, careful not to slip on any rocks or debris. Upon reaching Hurley, he sees that they are standing in front of a small opening - one of the caves, perhaps.

John calls out to his dog, "What is it Hurley, what do you see?" Hurley's tail wags in response, signaling that he has picked up on something. "Yes, I smell it too," John says to his faithful companion. He takes a few deep breaths, trying to detect the same scent that Hurley must have picked up on from the opening of the cave. All he can smell is a faint musty odor, like stale air. But Hurley must have sensed something else. Just as John thinks this to himself, Hurley begins to growl and bare his teeth, his fur standing on end in a defensive stance. John gently pets his head and reassures him, "It's okay boy, take it easy." As he reaches down to take hold of Hurley's collar and lead him away from the cave, he notices how tense and scared he seems.

"Let's go, boy," John says, urging Hurley on as they make their way towards the creek. Hurley gets excited and starts splashing around, even jumping back when he encounters a rock in the water. John looks for the source of the rock, but finds nothing except for Hurley playfully rolling around in the grass. As they continue walking, John admires the peaceful-ness of the trees and the fresh air. Suddenly, his tranquility is broken by a voice yelling at him to stay away. The sound echoes through the area, causing John to jump and his adren-aline to kick in. He searches for the source of the voice, but sees nothing except for a boulder tumbling down from an old homestead and into the creek. Just as he thinks it couldn't get any stranger, he hears a deep growling coming from across the creek. Turning around, he sees Hurley staring intently.

"Come on, Hurley! Let's go!" John shouts to his dog, but Hurley continues to growl. This is a new sound for him, and it sends chills down John's spine. Hurley's body language is also concerning; he looks ready to pounce. John tries to take his collar and lead him away, but Hurley refuses to move. John decides to start up the mule in hopes that the noise will distract Hurley and it worked. He heard John speeding away in the Kawasaki Mule and Hurly bolted right after him.

As they head down the logging road towards their camper, Hurley suddenly runs ahead and scares up a rabbit from the tall grass.

John can't shake off the feeling of unease as he drives back to the camper. He can't help but think about the mysterious voice he heard earlier and where it might have come from. Something just doesn't feel right about this place. It could be related to the human finger he found in the old homestead, or maybe there's something lurking in that cave. He resolves to bring a camera and flashlight with him next time he goes exploring with Hurley.

After lunch, John pulls up in front of the Beaver Creek Sheriff's department and walks inside. He introduces himself and explains that he found a human finger with a wedding ring still attached on his property. The sheriff confirms that it is indeed a human phalange and suggests setting up wildlife cameras near the cave to potentially capture any activity. John confirms he has been doing that.

"So, it seems. Sheriff, would you be able to conduct a test on the bone to determine its age?"

"Yes, Mr. Smith, we can send it off for DNA testing. I'll also need you to take my deputy out to the area where you found the finger so he can gather more evidence. This could potentially be a crime scene."

"Sheriff, this is an old homestead, and I would prefer to preserve it in its original state as much as possible. You aren't planning on digging up the entire property, are you?"

"That will depend on what we find and the results of our tests. Where exactly did you find this little finger?"

"It was on my property. Like I mentioned before, I only purchased it a few months ago...the Old Saxon estate."

"Oh, you mean Martha Saxon's place over on Sulfur Mountain?"

"Yes, Sheriff."

"I know exactly which property you're referring to. The old homestead by the creek, correct? That's the Stellar homestead. Has anyone told you about its history, Mr. Smith?"

"No, Sheriff. Is there something I should know?"

"Well, there have been plenty of strange stories circulating throughout the years about that property and what has happened there. I suggest you prepare yourself for some surprises. Perhaps do some research at the local library in Beaver Creek about the families who owned that property. It has a lot of history and tales even more twisted than those of the Brothers Grimm put together! Looks like some of them are finally coming to light."

# 3

## "FOLKLORE"

It's 5:30 am on a chilly October morning when Victor arrives at Nell's Diner. The snow is falling, and the temperature is a frigid 25 degrees. As he parks his car, he can't help but think that it's not a good day to sell real estate in Eastern Kentucky. However, he has more pressing matters to attend to at the office. Recently, there has been an increase in inquiries about foreclosed farms in the Beaver Creek area, and Victor needs to handle these emails before they pile up.

He steps out of his car and grabs his newspaper and scarf before making his way into Nell's Diner. The owners, Nell, and Ed, greet him with warm smiles as he takes a seat in the far back corner of the cozy establishment. With its limited seating for about 50 people, the diner exudes a quaint charm reminiscent of the 1950s. Elvis memorabilia lines the walls, which is

Ed's pride and joy. Nell, who is in her mid-fifties like Ed, is known for her genuine hospitality and kind demeanor that draws customers in. Despite his gruff exterior, Ed is a softie at heart and even plays Santa Claus for the town every Christmas.

As he settles into his booth, Victor realizes that despite the rough weather outside, coming to Nell's always brings warmth and comfort. It's no wonder why it's a favorite among locals and visitors alike.

Nell mentions that Ed dreads this time of year because he must put aside his tough demeanor and act jolly and kind to everyone. Nell always chuckles when she tells the stories of Ed playing Santa for Beaver Creek. There's even a display of photos on the wall next to the restrooms.

Nell approaches Victor to take his breakfast order. "Would you like your usual or would you like to try Ed's special today?"

"I'll take a chance and try Ed's special today."

"I heard that, Victor!" Ed shouts from the small kitchen in the diner.

"Be careful, Victor. Ed's in a bad mood today," Nell whispers.

"Oh, he knows I'm just teasing him. Someone has to keep him in line around here."

Victor says loud enough for Ed to hear him. Nell laughs as she pours him a cup of hot coffee.

"Your breakfast will be ready soon, dear," Nell says before going to serve another customer who just sat down at the bar counter.

Victor waits for his food and reads today's newspaper. On the front page, he sees a headline about another missing girl. A photo accompanies the article, showing a young blonde girl with blue eyes and a sweet smile wearing a pink shirt with "Love 01" written on it. The Sheriff is asking anyone with information about her whereabouts to contact the Beaver Creek Sheriff's office. The article explains that her name is Abigail Flynn, a local high school student who went camping on Beaver Creek with friends. The last time anyone saw her was when she went into her tent with her boyfriend, whose name cannot be released due to being underage at seventeen years old or younger according to the parents' request.

Rumors are spreading in town about the missing girls from Beaver Creek. They disappear without a trace, and no one knows who took them or how. The community has formed a search party to look for Abigail, the latest girl to vanish. Her mother mentions that she always kept her cell phone close, but it was missing when she disappeared. The police suspect foul play. Nell offers Victor a refill on his coffee and notices he's reading about Abigail's disappearance in the newspaper. She comments on the ongoing pattern of disappearances near the caves in Beaver Creek and laments that some people still don't stay away from the dangerous area. Nell also mentions rumors that the spirit of Anne Stellar, an alleged witch who was burned at the stake in 1849, or her husband's vengeful ghost may be responsible for these tragedies due to their brutal deaths at the hands of townspeople.

"He threatened to seek revenge on each and every family member who played a part in Anne's burning and George's hanging," Nell recounted.

"Abigail Flynn is the 12th girl to go missing in the past decade. They say there has been a troubling number of unsolved disappearances in Beaver Creek since the deaths of Anne and George. Even the Marshal vanished one night while riding his horse home, leaving no trace except for the tied-up horse at the same tree where George was hung. It's eerie if you ask me. I wouldn't want to be related to any of those families. Who knows what could happen? There are rumors about those caves being Indian burial grounds for the Cherokee."

Victor grins at Nell and suggests, "Maybe there really are vengeful Indian spirits or ghosts lurking in those caves, taking anyone who trespasses on their land."

While Victor and Nell were discussing the missing girls, a man sitting behind them overheard their conversation. He chimed in, telling them about Benny Saxon, who supposedly still lives in the Devil's Attic and is no longer human. The man shared a story from years ago about his friend who went hunting for beavers near Beaver Creek and encountered something strange in one of the caves. As he cautiously explored the cave with his rifle, he heard a voice beckon him to come closer. Suddenly, he felt warm breath on his neck and a hand with sharp nails grabbed him. In panic, the man fired off his rifle, revealing a creature that was neither human nor animal - it had glowing red eyes, slimy grayish-white skin, long claws, and sharp teeth. Scared out of his mind, the man broke free and ran away as fast as he could, never looking back until he reached safety. His friend claimed that the experience was so terrifying that he even soiled his pants. The man finished his story by saying that his friend described the creature as humanoid but not quite human, with features that he had never seen before.

My friend is not the type to make up stories, so when he told me he saw Benny Saxon attacked and survive in a dark cave by "selling his soul to the devil," I believed him. But when Victor asked if anyone had checked the cave for evidence, the man explained that it took some convincing before Dave allowed them to tell the sheriff. Even after a search was conducted, nothing was found - no footprints, no tracks, nothing. The official explanation was that Dave was drunk and imagined it all, but I know him better than that. He's perfectly sane. However, ever since the incident and the subsequent article in the paper labeling him as crazy, Dave has been struggling with the joke made at his family's expense.

Victor was entranced by the man's tale. He had knowledge of the events that take place in Devil's Attic, something that fascinated Victor. He often enjoys manipulating people and flying under the radar, keeping his thoughts hidden. This is a skill he has honed over a lifetime, appearing innocent and friendly on the surface while harboring hatred towards the people of Beaver Creek. He understands why the town blames George Stellar for their misfortunes because he too has a history with them, as did his mother. But that was many years ago, and now they do not even recognize him. Victor intends to keep it that way as he has only one goal that will keep him in Beaver Creek until it is accomplished.

# 4

## "STELLAR HOMESTEAD"

**BEAVER CREEK 1839**

"Push, Anne, push!" George's voice rings out, urgent and determined. "I can see the baby's head. It's almost here, but you must help me! Push with all your strength."

Anne obeys, letting out a piercing scream that echoes through the small cabin and could probably be heard in the nearest town 10 miles away.

"It's a girl! Mary, come look," George calls out to his older daughter. "You have a little sister. Here, take her while I help your mother clean up."

Mary carefully takes the newborn baby from her father's hands and wraps her in a soft blanket before settling by the fireplace. The cabin is a cozy two-story structure, with an open layout on the first floor consisting of a kitchen, living area, and a large hearth. The fireplace is big enough to cook over with hanging pots and herbs adorning the windows and doors. Made of granite from the nearby creek bed, it is the only source of warmth during Kentucky's harsh winter months.

The air inside is filled with the comforting scents of spices and burning wood, providing refuge from the raging snowstorm outside. The howling wind seems to surround the cabin, knocking against its walls like someone seeking entrance. But it is just tree branches being tossed about by the storm.

"Hi there, little one," Mary coos to her new sister as she rocks her gently. "My name is Mary, and you're my sister now. I think I'll call you Molly, okay? You look like a Molly to me."

Mary holds the newborn baby girl close to her chest, hoping to soothe her cries. She calls out to her mother Anne, asking for permission to feed her.

"Mom, can I feed Molly? She seems hungry," Mary says.

"Not yet Mary. Give me a few minutes and I'll take care of it," Anne responds. She makes her way over to the fireplace and sits down beside Mary and the baby.

"This is Molly," Mary introduces her mother to the baby in her arms.

"So, you've decided on Molly as her name?" Anne asks.

"Yes, ma'am. It suits her. She looks like a Molly," Mary explains.

"Well then, Molly it is. Molly Louise Stellar," Anne confirms with a smile.


### Summer 1848 Stellar Homestead

"Molly and Mary, would you like to help me protect the house with an enchantment?" Anne asked her two daughters.

"Yes, mother," Mary replied. "Come on, Molly, this will be fun."

Anne instructed them to gather the necessary items for the enchantment so they could begin.

"Okay, I need your help gathering some rosemary from the garden. And we'll also need some peas, sea salt, and brick powder for the bag," Anne said.

Molly carefully placed one pea at the edge of the house under Anne's guidance. "Right there is perfect, darling. Thank you," Anne told her.

"Mary, let's make a circle around the entire house with the brick dust. Good job. Now, both of you take some sea salt and rosemary and place it under every window on the ground, in a line with the salt," Anne instructed while she began to talk to the house herself.

Anne pulled out a piece of paper from her apron and unfolded it. She faced the cabin with the sun at her back and remembered exactly what needed to be done. She began to read aloud from the paper given to her by a woman in town. As she followed the directions, Anne thought about each item as she read. Meanwhile, Mary and Molly were completing their tasks - placing the salt around windows and doors. With her back still facing towards the sunlight, Anne began to recite the spell itself to cast protection over the house.

As Anne chants the spell, a soft breeze begins to blow. As she continues, the wind grows stronger and blows in all directions. She envisions an invisible shield surrounding their home, filled with protective energy.

*"I call upon the powers of the god and goddess,*

*My ancestors, my spirit that guides me,*
*Encircle my home with a protective energy*
*Keep all evil spirits away from this place*
*With the guidance of my spirit guides, ancestors, and gods, I erect a*
*strong invisible barrier around my house with these items I place*
*upon the foundation...."*

The wind suddenly stops, and the sun becomes blindingly bright, casting a warm glow over the area. Anne hesitates as she looks up at the light, closing her eyes to shield them. When she opens them again, the light has faded, and everything is back to normal.

"Okay Molly, place the last pea on this corner of the house. Our home is now protected from evil spirits." Anne crouches down and playfully chases the two girls around the house as they giggle and squeal. She catches Molly and lifts her up in a hug.

"No more nightmares, little one. This will make all those bad dreams go away."

Molly has been plagued by terrifying nightmares since she was only two years old. Anne hopes that the enchantment she obtained from a gypsy in town will convince her that their home is safe from any evil spirits. Molly's recurring nightmare involves someone burning down their cabin and killing her parents, something that has intensified as she's gotten older. It's been a constant struggle for Anne to find a solution - she's tried various calming herbs and even sought help from the Amish family nearby, but nothing seems to work. The local clerk at the general store suggested seeing the gypsy for a cure, and although Anne is not entirely convinced, she trusts her knowledge of herbs and is willing to try anything to finally put an end to Molly's nightmares.

"No more bad dreams, my dear. This will make them all go away."

### Spring 1849 Stellar Homestead

A knock on the door interrupts dinner. "I'll get it," Mary volunteers, but her husband George insists on answering the door himself. He reminds Mary not to answer the door without his permission. A voice calls out from outside, asking for Mr. Stellar. George confirms that he is indeed Mr. Stellar and asks what the matter is. The visitor introduces himself as Marshal Crane from the United States Marshal Service and says they need to speak with George's wife, Anne Stellar. George demands to know what this is about, but the Marshal demands to be let in to speak with Anne. George refuses and gets into a confrontation with the Marshal and his men who try to restrain him. Meanwhile, the Marshal calls out for Anne by name and barges into their home. He is described as a large man with an unruly appearance and cowboy attire, including a leather trench coat and spurs on his boots. Anne is frightened by his imposing presence.

"I'm Anne Stellar," she says, her voice trembling.

"Ma'am, I need you to come with us," the man in uniform states.

"Why?" Anne asks, fear evident in her voice.

"I'm asking for your cooperation, so we don't have to cause a scene in front of your children," he replies.

"No!" George shouts, coming to his wife's defense. "She's not going anywhere! Who do you think you are barging into my home like this?"

"Mrs. Stellar, it's up to you," the Marshal insists as he leads Anne away.

"Mary, take care of your sister while I'm gone. I'll go into town and figure out what's going on. I'll be back by morning. And remember, don't open the door for anyone!" George instructs.

Mary starts to cry. "Yes, Daddy. Please bring Mommy back."

"I'll be back soon, my darlings." George crouches down to hug both Molly and Mary tightly. He gives them a kiss before heading out the door. Racing into the town he sees a commotion going on. To his shock, he finds his wife Anne tied to a stake in front of the general store. George rushes over but is quickly grabbed by several men and pulled to the ground.

"What's going on? That's my wife! She hasn't done anything wrong! What is wrong with you people?" George screams and struggles to break free from their grasp.

"Mr. Stellar, your wife Anne has been found guilty of witchcraft," the Marshal informs him as everyone watches.

"What? What are you talking about? She's not a witch," George protests.

"Your wife has been seen trading herbs for spells with an old Gypsy lady."

"You're insane! Anne is not a witch."

"Set her on fire!" someone shouts from the crowd. "Burn the witch!" The chant spreads like wildfire through the onlookers. "Burn the witch, burn her to the ground!"

George's screams echo through the air as he watches helplessly as they prepare to set fire to his innocent wife.

In a neat pile around her, three men light the bottom of the wood. The stacked logs lead up to where Anne is bound and gagged, preventing her from casting spells on the townspeople. George watches as the flames grow higher, unable to bear the sight of his wife burning. One of the men forces George to look up at the fire, taunting him with, "Watch your witch burn!"

The Marshal approaches and hands George Anne's necklace, a heart-shaped locket with pictures of their daughter inside.

"I thought you might want this," he says.

George is still in disbelief over what has happened. Trying to make sense of this brutal act against his family, he looks up at the Marshal and declares, "I will get revenge on all those who took part in this heinous act against my loved ones."

"Is that a threat, Mr. Stellar?" asks the Marshal.

"Take it however you want but mark my words: your day will come, and I will be the one you beg for mercy from. Not your god, not your law, but me. And I will show none of you any mercy."

George breaks free from the grip of the men holding him and returns to his wagon. As he drives back home, he struggles with how to explain the senseless violence that just occurred to his young daughters. How can he tell them that their mother is gone? How can he answer their innocent questions?

"Molly, where's mommy?" his daughter asks.

"Mommy... your mother had... girls, please sit down. I have something difficult to tell you. Your mother won't be coming home."

"Why not, Daddy?"

"Well, there are rules we must follow in this land as people, and it's known as the law."

"What's the law, Daddy?"

"The law is a set of rules established by those in power that we must abide by. If we break these rules, we are punished."

"Is that why mommy isn't coming home? Because she broke the rules?"

"Yes, Molly, you could see it that way. The Marshal holds power in our area and he punished your mother for practicing witchcraft."

"Witchcraft?" Mary asked. "How so? Because she cast a spell on the house to ward off evil spirits?"

"What kind of spell did she use on the house?" George inquired.

"Last summer, Mother asked Molly and me to help her sprinkle brick dust, sea salt, rosemary, and peas around the house and under the windows. While we did that, she spoke some words to the house."

"What exactly did she say to the house?" George pressed.

"I don't remember all of it, but something about her spirit guiding and protecting the house from evil forces," replied Mary.

"She said it was to stop my nightmares, Daddy," Molly chimed in.

"Ah, so she was trying to keep the evil spirits away that were causing Molly's bad dreams. And did it work?"

"Yes, Daddy. I haven't had that dream since then," Molly answered.

"Well then, it must have worked," George concluded with a smile.

Molly awoke with a blood-curdling scream, causing George and Mary to jump from their slumber. George rushed down the hallway and noticed a burning smell coming from their cabin. As he investigated, he saw an orange glow outside the window. He quickly grabbed Molly and Mary and led them outside. Once they were safe, he went back inside to retrieve some blankets for the girls as they stood watching their cabin go up in flames. Shockingly, he realized that some people from town had intentionally set their home on fire.

Enraged, George confronted the Marshal and his deputies who were standing in the shadows, observing the destruction of their cabin. He threatened to kill them all for endangering his family's lives. The Marshal ordered his deputies to restrain George as he tried to defend himself. Then, he instructed them to take Molly and Mary to safety at the Church where the priest was waiting for them. Despite his anger, George knew it was best to follow the Marshal's orders for the sake of his daughters' safety, yet he knew it was wrong and had a bad feeling the girls wouldn't make it to the church.

"What do you mean he's waiting for them? Are you planning on burning them too? You're sick, Marshal. You don't follow any real law; you just make it up as you go along. You're nothing but a coward." "Mr. Stellar, you have been found guilty of harboring a witch, and the punishment is death by hanging. Would you like your daughters to witness this or would you prefer for the nuns to take care of them?"

"You're insane! I will get my revenge on you and your entire family. You'll all die one by one, and I will come back to take them. Just wait and see."

The Marshal orders his men to take George up to Sulfur Mountain and hang him. "Bring a rope and Mr. Stellar up that hill, tie it up high for him," he commands sternly. "I don't want anyone cutting him down or any wild animals getting to him."

"Yes, sir Marshal."

"Leave him there for the crows to deal with."

BELLA FROST

# 5

## "JOHN SMITH"

JOHN SMITH RETURNS to his property after a few months away. He had left for the holidays to spend time with his wife and two sons in Colorado. Before returning home, he also had to fly to Asia to fix some industrial conveyor machines for his business. Despite living in Colorado, John also owns houses in Vancouver, Canada and will soon have one in Kentucky as well. His company has 25 employees and provides services for industrial conveyor machines all over the world, including designing programs, updates, and repairs.

John's family consists of his wife Elizabeth (Lizzie for short) and their two sons, Jake, and Kyle. John graduated from MIT with a master's degree in EECS (Electrical Engineering & Computer Science), where he finished at the top of his class with honors. He is an only child; both of his parents passed away in a boating accident when he was 27.

As John makes his way back to his property, he loads the mule with outdoor cameras that he plans to mount on the land. His dog Hurley runs alongside him with boundless energy - a mix of Australian Shepherd and Burmese Mountain Dog.

After spending a week fixing fences, laying new ones, and cutting down trees, John checks the SD cards on his trail cameras to see if they captured any interesting footage. The first camera he looks at is positioned near an old foundation and another towards a cave entrance where Hurley seemed agitated during their last visit.

"Look at all of these photos, Hurley!" John exclaims to his loyal companion. He walks over to the camera facing the cave and realizes it has taken over 100 pictures. "That must be a lot of beavers or deer out here," he thinks to himself.

He returns to his mule and sets off to check the other cameras he placed along the property line - some facing outside of the property, others inside. Each one has images on its SD card. By the time John gets back to his camper, it is almost dark with a beautiful sunset.

After dinner, John pulls out his laptop and inserts the first SD card. He can't wait to see what was captured on the camera facing the cave. As he loads the images onto his computer, he notices the first few are of deer and beavers swimming in the creek and building their dam downstream. There are also plenty of shots of wild turkeys and a family of bobcats. But as more photos load, most of them are dark with white blurs - something moving quickly in front of the camera. Some even have long white streaks as if something flew by. John considers that it might just be fog triggering the cameras but then notices something strange in one of the last photos: an odd figure in the opening of the cave. He zooms in for a closer look.

"What is that red light in the cave?" John speaks to himself, his voice echoing in the quiet room. He zooms in with his camera and sees two glowing red eyes on a grey figure emerging from the mouth of the cave. The camera must have taken a photo, startling whatever it was as it looked directly at the lens before disappearing back into the darkness. John leans back in his chair, shocked by what he has just seen.

"Holy shit, what could be out there?" he mutters to himself.

He quickly scrolls through the rest of the images on the disk's, but the strange figure does not appear in any of them. Moving on to the next SD card, which contains photos from the Stellar Foundation site, John eagerly waits for them to load. But again, he only sees familiar animals like deer, beaver, bobcat, and turkey, along with some white streaks. However, with this new camera's higher resolution, the white streaks are more defined and resemble a person made of fog or smoke with amber eyes. Suddenly, the figure disappears in a flash of white streaks, seemingly moving all over the forest and creek below.

John continues searching through each SD card, only to find similar results - more white streaks and plenty of wildlife captured on camera. Feeling frustrated and confused, he shuts down his computer and stands up to get a drink of water. As he passes by the kitchen window, something catches his eye in the field outside. He quickly turns to get a closer look and sees that a thin layer of snow has covered everything in sight, making it look smooth and ethereal under the bright moonlight.

John fixates on the dark figure in the distance, a dark figure that appears to be a tall human standing there. He can't believe what he's seeing and waits for it to move or disappear. As he moves from the kitchen window to the living room, he notices other dark figures surrounding the larger one in the center. He questions if this is reality or bizarre dream. The figure starts making its way towards his camper and John quickly grabs his rifle from behind the chair. Opening the front door, he shines a flashlight across the field, but whatever was there has vanished. Hurley, his dog, joins him and they cautiously walk down the steps together, scanning their surroundings. They find nothing except fresh snow covering any potential footprints. Suddenly, a loud scream breaks through the silence, causing John to freeze in fear. He can tell it's not a human scream and he starts heading back to his camper when he sees another dark figure inside, staring back at him from within.

John stood frozen in terror, his mind racing as he tried to process what was happening. The looming figure before him had no distinguishable features, just a tall black silhouette that seemed to be wearing some sort of hat.

Without thinking, John takes off running towards the camper and sees the figure moving away from the window. He calls out for Hurley, hoping his dog will come to his aid. As he approaches the camper, Hurley jumps up inside and growls.

John cautiously makes his way up the steps, pausing briefly to take a deep breath before entering. Suddenly, Hurley bursts out of the camper and John turns to see where he went. Shining his flashlight around, he sees Hurley's footprints in the snow and follows them down to the edge of the nearby field. He can hear him barking, he yells for him, but the dog keeps running after something. John rushes back to get the mule. Putting his rifle and flashlight in the front passenger seat he floors the gas spinning dirt as he rushes to find Hurley's tracks in the soft blanket of snow.

The prints lead John to an old Stellar foundation, and he can hear Hurley barking in the distance. Ignoring the freezing cold water, John wades through thigh-deep water of the creek to get to the other side where he spots Hurley barking near a cave entrance. Fueled by adrenaline and fear for his beloved pet,

John runs towards the cave and calls out for Hurley as he approaches its dark opening.

"Hurley, are you in there?" John calls out into the cave.

He can hear Hurley whimpering and barking frantically, as if something is wrong. Reluctantly, John enters the narrow opening of the cave, his heart racing with fear. As he walks further inside, the cave twists around several large columns before finally opening into a larger room. The ceiling stretches high above him, dripping with water that echoes off the walls. In the dim light of his flashlight, John can see cave crickets chirping and a still pool of water to his left that looks like glass.

But as he continues deeper into the cave, it starts to narrow again until he must crawl through a small tunnel. On the other side, he sees Hurley cowering down in fear, almost as if he's done something wrong. "It's okay boy," John says soothingly as he approaches Hurley. But Hurley just lies there, refusing to get up or move. Concerned, John checks him over for any injuries but finds nothing. He tries to coax Hurley to come with him by tapping his leg, but Hurley still won't budge. Finally, he stands up and looks towards the darkness behind them with fearful eyes. Following his gaze, John lifts his flashlight and sees an unknown object lying on the cave floor ahead of them. "What is that?" He whispers to himself as he cautiously makes his way towards it.

John's sudden outburst of "Oh my god!" echoes through the cave, startling Hurley. How did she get in here? His flashlight reveals the body of a young girl, half-buried in mud and dirt, naked and missing body parts. She must have been here for months, maybe even longer.

"Good boy, Hurley. We need to go get the Sheriff," John says as he pats his faithful dog on the head.

As they start to make their way back towards the entrance of the cave, John notices a set of footprints that don't belong to him or Hurley. He quickly scans the cave with his light but doesn't see or hear anything except for the sound of water dripping from the ceiling.

"Let's go, Hurley." They both exit the cave and return to their camper.

Walking to the camper John realizes that he had left the door open. He cautiously walks around the camper, checking for any signs of someone or something else being inside. He sees Hurley rolling around on the rug and calls out to him to wait until he gets a towel.

"It's almost 3:15 am. We'll wait and call the Sheriff in the morning. We need some rest first, right boy?" John asks Hurley before settling down for the night.

# 6

## "BODY OF THE GIRL"

"Hello, I would like to speak with Sheriff Taylor. Is he available?

"Of course, may I ask who is calling?

"This is John Smith."

"Hi Mr. Smith, this is Sheriff Taylor speaking."

"Sheriff, I need your help. I found a body of a young girl in one of the caves on my property last night."

"I see. Please stay where you are, and we will come out to you as soon as possible."

When Sheriff Taylor and Deputy Ward arrive at John's camper, John greets them outside. The Sheriff is cautious and unsure about the situation, considering there have been 12 young girls reported missing in the area without any leads. They all disappeared near Beaver Creek, which borders John's property. John explains what he found and requests to show the Sheriff where he discovered the dismembered body in the cave. The Sheriff informs John that a girl has been missing for about 4 months after camping with friends nearby. They questioned her boyfriend at the time but did not find any connection to her disappearance.

"Please show us exactly where you were when you found the body, Mr. Smith."

They follow the path down to the creek, which has significantly decreased in water level since the previous night.

"Sheriff, you'll have to cross the creek to get to her," John informs him as they make their way through the cave. John leads the way with a flashlight, and they eventually arrive at a woman's body.

"Any idea who she is or how she ended up here?" John asks the Sheriff.

"Deputy Ward, can you light some flares so we can see better?" The Sheriff directs. And everyone, please don't touch anything. This is now a crime scene, and I'll need Mr. Smith to stay put until this is resolved. Don't plan on leaving town either just in case I have more questions for you."

"Yes, Sheriff. I wasn't planning on leaving until I finished installing the fence and gates anyway," Mr. Smith replies.

"Well, you might be staying longer than intended then. Please go back to your camper and stay there for now," the Sheriff instructs.

John heads back to the camper to wait for the Sheriff's further instructions. But upon arriving, he decides to go back out and put the SD cards back in the cameras. He remembers that none of them had any cards in them last night. There could be vital footage on one of them if they were installed correctly. After replacing all the cards, he returns to find Sheriff Taylor waiting for him at the camper.

"Didn't I tell you to stay still, Mr. Smith?"

"I just went out on the property to put my SD cards back in all the cameras I have placed around the property."

"You have cameras on your property?"

"Yes sir, I put up wildlife cameras to capture any activity in the cave and observe the wildlife in the area."

"That's a smart move, Mr. Smith. Have you found anything yet?"

"Just some blurry images of animals and a figure that looks human but with red glowing eyes."

"Are you trying to pull my leg, Mr. Smith?"

"No sir, Sheriff."

"Do you know that old Dave told me the same story years ago when he was in that cave? And now you're saying you have a picture of this creature? I'd like to see it because I thought Dave was crazy."

John invites Sheriff Taylor into his camper and opens his laptop to show him the pictures from the SD card. He points out all the blurry streaks and then the one clear image of a humanoid figure with grayish skin and red eyes.

"Well, I'll be damned! Look at that! I can hardly believe it!" The Sheriff stands there with his mouth open, rubbing his head in disbelief.

"Do you have any idea what those white streaks could be?" The Sheriff asks John.

"No, sir. I don't," John replied.

"I'll tell you what those ghostly white streaks are. This land was once a burial ground for the Cherokee Indians who settled here hundreds of years ago. They've discovered arrowheads, pottery, artifacts, and bones all over the area along Beaver Creek. The tribe used to take shelter in the caves and would hold ceremonies to honor their deceased members by burning them. They believed this would help their spirits find their way to the afterlife and become their spirit animal. I never believed in any of that nonsense, but your pictures provide some compelling evidence."

"Who is the young girl, Sheriff?" John inquired.

"I hate to say it, but I think it might be Abigail Flynn, the girl who has been missing for a couple of months now. We'll have to wait for CSI to examine all the evidence and confirm."

The Sheriff left, and John went back to work on the fences. It has been a few weeks since then, and the Sheriff has been checking in on him regularly, hoping for an explanation other than a Native American spirit. But so far, nothing out of the ordinary has shown up on his cameras except for more white streaks appearing throughout the forest surrounding the field. The activity around each camera has also increased, with some even being destroyed. In response, John mounted additional video cameras around his camper to capture any sightings of the black figure again.

John wakes up to the sound of loud knocking and banging on his camper. His dog Hurley growls, but John hushes him so he can listen carefully. He can hear multiple voices outside, talking all at once like a bustling restaurant. John gets out of bed and checks the cameras that monitor the perimeter of his camper. Without turning on any lights or making noise, he observes white streaks moving rapidly in different directions outside. As he watches each camera feed, he notices these spirits seem to be Native American in origin and they appear to be angry with him. The force of their pounding shakes the camper's roof, walls, doors, and windows. John hopes nothing will break as one of the spirits stops in front of the camera. It resembles a wolf head with a human body, its eyes suddenly glowing bright yellow before darting away. John is astonished by what he sees and feels relieved that he has recorded it for proof. He had hooked up a recorder just in case something like this happened and now he is glad he did. The white streaks eventually pause and stare directly into the cameras, almost as if they know John is watching them. One by one, he identifies each creature - a crow, a bear, a wolf, a coyote, a panther, and an eagle - all with human-like bodies but animal heads made of wispy white smoke.

After several minutes of watching and waiting, the mysterious figures suddenly disappear. John peers out the window, but there's no sign of them. Puzzled, he settles back into his chair and continues to monitor the area. Soon, he notices movement in the distance, coming closer to the camper from across the field. It appears to be floating and moving rapidly towards them.

"Oh my god, it's that black figure again," John exclaims as he watches on the monitor. The figure is solid black with no discernible features except for two glowing red eyes that seem to stare directly at him. He can feel his fear growing as the figure gets closer and closer.

Suddenly, an arm emerges from its side, holding something up in the air. John zooms in on the monitor to get a better look and realizes with horror that it's a human skull. As if sensing his terror, the figure lifts another arm and reveals a human head.

"What does it want?" John mutters to himself in fear. He continues to watch as the figure turns and moves towards a nearby cave, going in the opposite direction from where it came. "It must be trying to tell me something," John thinks to himself. He pats Hurley, his loyal dog, who has been watching intently by his side.

"I need to place a camera near Devil's Attic cave," John realizes. "Maybe that's where this creature is coming from."

# 7

## "THE EVIDENCE"

JOHN STARTLES awake and jumps out of bed, realizing it's already 8:00 am. He scolds his dog Hurley for sleeping in and not waking him up at their usual time of 5:30 am. John quickly gets dressed and gathers the taped recordings from last night, eager to show them to the Sheriff.

As they head into town in John's truck with Hurley, they pass by a diner that catches John's eye. The sign boasts about their burgers, tempting him to stop there for lunch later. When he arrive at the Sheriff's office, John notices a couple of CSI investigators walking towards them. He greets the Sheriff and presents the recordings from his video cameras he installed outside his camper. The Sheriff leads them all to the conference room where they can watch the footage on a TV and disc player.

The group enters the conference room, and the Sheriff shuts the door behind them. John glances back to see that more CSI investigators already waiting inside.

"Don't be alarmed, John. I requested their presence," the Sheriff explains.

"It's no problem," John replies.

He inserts a media device into the player while the Sheriff turns on the TV. They take seats at the table and begin watching the recordings. For the first ten or fifteen minutes, all they see is darkness.

"I hope it gets more interesting than this, John," the Sheriff comments.

John laughs and responds, "It does. Do you have a remote we can use to fast-forward?"

"Somewhere in here... ah, here it is."

The Sheriff hands John the remote and he skips ahead until they reach a point where motion sensor lights are triggered. Suddenly, white streaks resembling fog appear in the footage, blowing across the field. John pauses and plays the tape at normal speed. The fog seems to be gathering in the middle of the field, growing thicker and closer to their campsite. Then, there is a loud bang and one of the cameras begins to shake. A white streak zooms past it into the field. Another bang follows as more ghostly streaks head towards the fog in the distance.

As the fog begins to shift, everyone observes as it breaks into individual white streaks. These slender forms quickly dart around the field, up and down, back, and forth, until every trace of mist has vanished. Suddenly, there is a loud banging on the roof of the camper before it moves down to the windows and doors. Then, just as suddenly, it stops. One of the cameras captures footage of a white fog forming into a wolf-like creature with human features. Its eyes glow with an amber yellow hue as it stares directly at the camera.

"It's looking right at me!" one of the CSI agents exclaims. But just as quickly as it appeared, the creature disappears.

"Did you create that on your computer? It was amazing!" another agent asks.

"No, that's what comes onto my property at night," John replies calmly.

He explains that other creatures also appear in addition to the wolf, such as an eagle, a crow, a coyote, a bear, and a panther. Suddenly all the streaks fly towards the center and disappear into the ground within seconds. "It must be hiding in there somewhere," John says quietly.

All eyes are glued to the screen, waiting for the black figure to appear. After ten minutes, the motion lights turn off and the footage goes dark.

"It's here. I saw it last night, I swear Sheriff. I'm not making this up!" John insists, trying to convince the sheriff of his experience.

But after reviewing the tape again, the Sheriff can't find any evidence of the black figure.

"I'm sorry, John. The tape only shows white streaks. I wish I could have seen this figure holding two skulls as you described."

Disappointed, the Sheriff suggests that they bring in CSI experts to analyze the footage. He also asks John to accompany them to their lab for foot impressions to rule out any suspicions.

"My feet?" John questions.

"Yes, we need to eliminate any potential suspects," the Sheriff explains.

John recalls seeing another set of boot prints in the cave where he saw the figure and mentions it to the Sheriff.

"That's correct, John. We also found human footprints in the cave during our investigation. It could be from the missing girl or someone else."

"Okay, no problem. I understand," John agrees.

After putting his boots back on, he approaches the clerk at the front desk.

"Is there any way I could get information about an item I dropped off with Sheriff Taylor for a DNA test about six months ago?"

"Certainly. Just give me your name and a brief description of the item," replies the clerk.

"My name is John Smith and I dropped off a human finger bone with a ring on it. I found it on my new property," John explains.

"Well, this is certainly an interesting discovery on your newly acquired property, Mr. Smith. We had to send your file to Virginia for testing due to the age of the item. It seems that they are still not showing as available for viewing, even though the tests have been completed. Let me check with my supervisor, I'll be right back."

John waits at the desk while thoughts from last night swirl in his mind. What could have happened to the recording? He remembers watching it carefully and now the Sheriff probably thinks he's making things up. Next time, he'll need to buy a digital camera and take pictures when it shows up at the camper.

The clerk returns with her supervisor, Mrs. Nichols.

"Hello Mr. Smith, I am Mrs. Nichols. I looked up your file and spoke with the Virginia office. I have some information for you, and some strange findings that may make sense in a way. Firstly, the bone was dated back to the 1600s, possibly even earlier or slightly later. And there was a ring found on the finger which we enhanced and discovered an inscription on it. The language appears to be Romanian, also traced back to the 1600s. Our investigator did some research and found out what it means. Here's a copy."

"It was a spell. An immortality spell that said.....

"Even after death, the spirit will continue to wander among the living on this earth for as long as it desires!"

"That's both creepy and intriguing," John comments to Mrs. Nichols.

"Now the story gets even stranger, Mr. Smith. The woman who was in possession of this finger and ring has fallen ill and hasn't returned to complete the necessary paperwork."

"What kind of illness is it?"

"We don't know, and apparently no one else does either. She became sick shortly after receiving the item and taking off the ring to begin testing. Two weeks later she came into work, but her supervisor sent her home and told her to see a doctor.

According to her coworkers, she looked extremely ill and was constantly vomiting. Her doctor admitted her to the hospital for further tests. That night, her condition took a turn for the worse, and by the end of the week she had fallen into a coma. It's been four months now, and she's still unconscious. The strange part is, her supervisor told me that every night, she repeats the words 'Mona the great gypsy I call upon you please help'. The bone and ring are currently in quarantine, and no one can touch them due to what happened to the woman."

"I understand. Oh, my goodness! I hope she will recover. I feel awful now."

"Don't worry, Mr. Smith. We can't confirm if that's the cause of her illness yet. I'll keep you updated as soon as I have any news. Please leave your contact information with our recep-tionist Luan and have a good day, Mr. Smith."

"Thank you, Mrs. Nichols."

# 8

## "TRESPASSER'S"

AFTER PURCHASING a new digital camera in town, John returns to his camper at the homestead. Weeks pass without any issues until he takes a trip down to Devil's Attic and smells smoke in the air. Curiosity getting the best of him, John gets out of his mule and walks up to check the SD card on his camera. As he approaches the edge of the cliff, he sees several smoldering campfires below. Deciding to investigate further, he makes his way down and discovers trash left behind but no sight of any campers.

John jumps back into his mule and heads towards Beaver Creek to see if there are any campfires still burning there. As he nears the creek, he can smell more smoke and realizes it is not from downstream. Annoyed, he gets out of the mule and walks towards the beach area by the creek where he finds even more campfires on both sides of the creek and down the stream. Frustrated with what he sees, John wonders why anyone would be camping on his land without permission trashing the place and digging in the old foundation that don't belong to them. He angrily rubs his goatee and heads back to his mule, determined to figure out who these trespassers are.

After arriving at the camper and taking a moment to cool off, John decides to check on the progress of the construction workers building his large 7500 square foot steel garage. He's eager for it to be completed so he can protect his mule and camper from the unpredictable weather while he's away working in Colorado. Approaching the group of workers, John asks the supervisor how much longer until they finish.

"About a week, sir. We'll have it completely done," the supervisor replies confidently.

"That's great news. If you or your team need anything, just let me know. I'm always here on the property," John says with a friendly smile.

"Thank you, Mr. Smith."

Heading back into his camper, John reaches for his cell phone to call Sheriff Taylor and discuss the issue of trespassers on his property. As he goes to dial, he notices eight missed calls on his phone. Quickly scrolling through them, he sees that one of the missed calls was from Sheriff Taylor himself.

"Just the man I wanted to speak with," John thinks too himself as he goes to return the call. But before he can even press send; his phone begins to ring.

"Hello Sheriff Taylor? Perfect timing, I was just about to call you," John greets him.

"I'm glad I caught you John. There's something I need to tell you," Sheriff Taylor interrupts him before he can explain what he found on his property earlier.

"John, have you spoken to any newspapers?"

"I'm sorry, I don't understand."

"Have you read any newspapers recently?"

"No Sheriff, I don't subscribe to any."

"Have you been in contact with anyone from the newspapers about the situation on your property?"

"No Sheriff, I wouldn't do that. That's why I called you. I discovered several campfires and litter in the creek and caves...on my property!"

"I suspected this might happen."

"What do you mean by that, Sheriff?"

"Someone has found out about the paranormal activity on your property and the body of a girl found in the cave. They leaked it to the newspapers, and they've been publishing stories all weekend about it. It's chaos here in the office."

"Well, it's chaos here too. They left behind trash and campfires everywhere. How can we find out who leaked this information and how can I prevent anyone else from coming onto my property?"

"I don't think you'll have much luck keeping them off your property, John. It's like an open invitation now. My advice is to keep a close watch on them and put up some No Trespassing signs. If they threaten your safety, you have every right to handle the situation until backup arrives. But don't try to chase them off alone; it could get dangerous with just a group of young people out there.

"That's just great. Can't you send someone out here to remove them?"

"I could, but they'll probably just come back and cause more damage. Oh, and one more thing, John. You're in the clear for the boot and footprint impressions we found. One was yours going in and out, but the other boot and footprint belong to someone else. We still haven't identified them yet, but I'll let you know when we do. And remember, be gentle with those kids down there. Let the Native American spirits take care of them; they did a good job with you. Who knows, they might even provide some evidence of paranormal activity."

# 9

## "TORI"

WE URGENTLY NEED to find a gas station. Ashley, please use your phone to locate the nearest one. You're always on it playing games anyway.

"What's wrong, Curt? Do we really need gas?

"Yes, that's why I asked you to find a gas station."

"You should have stopped earlier like I suggested."

"We didn't need gas then, Ashley. Why would I stop?"

"To top off the tank so we wouldn't be in this situation, obviously!

"Whatever."

"Okay, it looks like there's a station about 30-45 minutes ahead. It's a Cumberland Farms store in Somerset, Kentucky. Do we have enough gas to get there?"

"I think so. That should be around 60 miles or less. Thanks for checking, Ashley."

"Yeah, whatever!"

They pull into the Cumberland Farms store to fill up on gas. Curt tells Ashley to wake up the others and see if they want anything. After stretching their legs and grabbing some snacks for their camping trip at Beaver Creek, they all gather back into the van one by one. Bryan asks Curt how much longer until they reach the cave at Beaver Creek.

"It's about an hour away from here," Curt replies. "We should arrive around 2:30 am."

It's early Friday morning and they all hope to capture some photos of ghosts and paranormal activity at the cave. They've brought along video equipment, cameras, and voice recorders in hopes of breaking into paranormal research with this first adventure in the Beaver Creek area and township.

As they turn onto Hwy 167, Brenda notices a charming little diner on the right.

"Nell's Diner. That looks like it would be a great spot for break-fast. I wonder what time they open?"

They all gaze at the diner as they pass by, imagining plates of eggs, bacon, hash browns, and toast with a refreshing glass of juice.

Lost in their thoughts, they find themselves turning onto a dirt path. As they slowly make their way down the path, they see cars parked on grassy embankments everywhere.

They can't believe how many people are here. Curt pulls up onto the grass to park the van. As he turns off the headlights, a dark figure suddenly jumps into the bushes.

"Did you see that?"

"Yes, what was that?" Ashley exclaims.

"Probably just someone's dog," Bryan replies.

"Yeah, maybe it's lost," Curt adds.

They all get out of the van and start grabbing their gear and bags. Bryan, Brenda, Katelyn, Jeff, Holly, Ashley, and Curt make their way towards Beaver Creek with excitement, eager to set up and start filming. Curt slows his pace as the others pass the area where the black figure had jumped into the bushes. He peers into the woods as he walks slower and eventually comes to a stop. Turning to face the direction of the figure, he thinks he sees something black moving between the trees in the distance. The full moon provides just enough light for him to navigate without a flashlight; he can see something dark moving in the distance.

"Hey there boy, are you lost?" Curt calls out softly towards it.

The dark object stops and turns towards him. Curt's heart starts racing at the thought that it might not be someone's dog after all; it could be a coyote or other wild animal. He stares at the figure as its eyes begin to glow red in the moonlight. Curt takes a sharp breath in fear.

Curt takes a few steps back, his eyes widening in shock. He turns to talk to his friends, but they are nowhere to be seen. How long have I been standing here, staring at this strange creature in the woods?

When he looks back, it's gone. Worried and confused, Curt starts walking down the path until he reaches a fork in the road. Which way did they go? He strains his ears for any signs of his friends talking, but all he can hear is the rustling of leaves. Suddenly, a loud growl startles him from behind. His body freezes with fear and his heart races faster. He tries to calm himself by taking deep breaths and counting to five before turning around to face whatever is making that noise. Slowly, he sees the outline of a human form behind him.

He spins around, expecting to see something terrifying, but instead, he sees the most beautiful girl he's ever laid eyes on. Her bright blue eyes, perfect curves, and lilac dress with orchid patterns make him drop his gear bag and gape at her in awe. Is this real or just a dream? She introduces herself as Tori and asks if he's okay. Still entranced by her beauty, Curt stammers out a response.

Tori mentions that many people have been coming here to find ghosts in the woods, reminding Curt of why he came in the first place. But now all thoughts of ghosts are forgotten as he gets lost in Tori's eyes and wonders how she suddenly appeared here.

As Tori approaches Curt, she asks, "What brings you here?"

She must look up at him, as he is taller than her with light brown hair and brown eyes. Compared to her, he is thin and lacking in muscle. But she finds him attractive, nonetheless. They stand together, Tori at 5'5" and Curt at 6'3". She takes a step closer and looks into his eyes, then reaches for his hand.

"Someone as beautiful as you shouldn't be interested in someone like me," Curt says with surprise.

But Tori insists that she wants him and moves in closer. She puts her hands around his neck, and they start to kiss passionately. Curt can't believe this gorgeous woman is kissing him; she is the one he has dreamed about for years. She is everything he imagined as the perfect partner - the one he would find pleasure with when he was alone at night. But now, she is real. He thinks to himself as they continue to kiss. Tori grabs his manhood through his pants and strokes him, causing him to press himself against her with excitement.

She pulls away and whispers, "Come with me, my love. Let's make love under the moonlight." She leads him to an open field, ready to become one with him in body and soul.

Beneath the moonlight, he lay in the grass and admired her beautiful body as his hand caressed it gently. Her skin sparkled like glitter, almost hypnotizing to watch. It had a soft golden glow that seemed to radiate from within, absorbing the energy of the full moon. His hand followed the curves of her body, tracing down the small of her back with tender strokes.

Her skin was smooth and silky, like warm satin sheets on a summer night. Her hair cascaded in long, blue-black strands like fine silk. He leaned in to smell its floral scent, a mixture of roses, honeysuckle, and jasmine. Closing his eyes, he rubbed her hair against his cheek as a gentle breeze blew over them.

As he opened his eyes, he noticed goosebumps forming on her flawless back. He couldn't resist running his hand over her round and perfectly toned buttocks, feeling his desire grow with each touch.

He moved closer, planting kisses on her buttocks before making his way down to her inner thigh. She rolls over eagerly spread her legs to show him she wanted him to explore her most intimate area. With gentle bites and licks, he pleasured her until he found just the right spot with his finger, causing her to moan with delight.

He sheds his pants and slowly inches forward, lavishing kisses on every inch of her back as he penetrates her. She gasps for air, letting out high-pitched squeals of delight as he thrusts deeper and harder inside her. With each movement, the tightness of her walls only intensifies his pleasure, until they are completely consumed by the sensations.

She suddenly pulls away, causing him to slide out of her, She rises onto her knees again sliding his erection inside deeper, her desire for him almost palpable.

Moments before he reaches the point of release, he pulls back and lifts her off him for a few seconds as holds himself in check, denying himself a climax until she reaches her climax.

She leans down, he kisses her neck and bites down gently, gazing into her brilliant blue eyes that glimmer pink at their centers. She grabs onto him and bites down hard in ecstasy, he groans with pleasure. Unable to control himself any longer, he thrusts with her hard and fast, almost seeming to hurt her with the force of movements within her.

Another thrust with increasing force, as she dig her nails into his back. They grow longer and sharper, piercing his skin as she pushes them deeper. As the pleasure intensifies, her teeth transform into fangs and she starts sucking his blood with hungry eyes burning red.

He moans in ecstasy as he reaches his peak inside her, thrusting deeply into her pleasure zone. But suddenly, the pleasure turns to pain as he tries to pull away from her. Her legs, now elongated and wrapped around him like a snake, holding him tightly in place. She digs her fingers even deeper into his flesh until she has her whole hand under his skin.

Despite his struggles, she forces her tongue through his neck and into his throat, cutting off his air supply. She waits for him to collapse out of her grasp. His seed drips from inside her onto the ground.

With one final burst of strength, he screams as she turns his head forcing her long tongue into his mouth and sucks out his brain and spinal fluid. As he falls limp, she crushes his skull between her hands and licking up every drop before reverting to her human form with a satisfied smile on her face.

She retracts her tongue and shoves the lifeless body off her. Standing up, she surveys her surroundings before looking down at the dry shell of a human that used to be so full of life. It's hard to believe that this decrepit creature was only 21 years old, and just moments ago it was bringing her pleasure. She wipes her mouth with the back of her wrist, smearing the whitish-red fluid that drips from it. Her eyes still burn like hot coals, making everything around her appear distorted. She blinks a few times, trying to regain focus and her eyes turn into a bright pink hue, almost like a reflective color under black light. She closes them tightly for a moment before opening them again, finally able to see as humans do once more. Her eyes are now a stunning blue as she spots her spaghetti strap mini dress on the ground. She slips into it and pulls it up over her perfectly shaped body. One last look at the corpse she has left behind fills her with remorse, and she kneels beside it, placing a hand on what remains of the person she took from this world.

"Please forgive me for my actions. I am unable to control myself, as it is a consequence of my attraction to men. Our time together was enjoyable, and I will always carry your memory with me. Your presence brought me happiness and vitality."

She plucks a flower from the nearby field and gently rests it in Curt's lifeless hand. With a heavy heart, she rises and begins her journey towards Beaver Creek.

# 10

## "THE SEARCH"

"Where did Curt go? He was just behind us," Jeff asks Ashley.

"I'm not sure, but there seem to be more tents than I expected," Bryan replies as they stand at the edge of the creek, surveying their surroundings. People are scattered around in sleeping bags, tents, and blankets by campfires.

"We'll never find a spot with all these people crowding the area," Jeff exclaims loudly. Ashley hushes him, reminding him not to draw attention.

"Shh, we don't want to get kicked out. Keep your voice down," she scolds. Frustrated, she walks up the hill to get away from the noise. Brenda asks where she's going, and Ashley explains that she's going to look for Curt.

Ashley continues walking and calling out for Curt, but he is nowhere to be found. Confused and concerned, she returns to the creek and joins the others.

"I was just trying to be kind Curt when I came back to look for you. The least you could do is answer me," she shouted, her voice echoing through the quiet campground.

As the rest of the group works on setting up their tents at Beaver Creek, Brenda asks, "So, did you find him?"

"No," Ashley responds, disappointment evident in her voice. "I walked all the way to the van and called him, but he never answered."

"Maybe he found another girl and set up camp further down the creek," Jeff suggests. "You'll have to wait until morning to see which tent, he's in."

"Yeah, I guess you're right. Goodnight everyone. See you in a few hours."

The next morning, with sunlight streaming through the trees above their campsites, Ashley frantically searches for her friend Curt. She runs to Bryan and Brenda's tent first, then makes her way to the last tent, unzipping the door and peering inside. She notices that his sleeping bag and the camping light she left on for him are untouched.

"Ashley, did you find him?" Bryan asks.

"No guys, I can't find him anywhere. He didn't even come back to sleep in his tent."

They all gather outside as Ashley checks his tent again, hoping to find some sign of Curt.

Ashley's voice was shaking as she pleaded with them to help find him. She desperately tried to wipe away the tears streaming down her face, refusing to believe that he could have just disappeared without a trace. Jeff tried to calm her down, insisting that he was probably just out having a good time with other people. After all, he was a smooth talker and had a natural charm that drew people in.

After a few minutes, Ashley headed towards the creek, determined to find some answers. Holly and Brenda followed behind, asking where she was going. She explained her plan to ask around the campsite near the creek if anyone had seen him. And if she found him, she was going to give him a piece of her mind for worrying her so much. The other girls decided to join her in the search.

"He could at least answer my calls or leave a message," Ashley complained as they walked. They approached a couple coming from the opposite direction and asked if they had seen him.

Ashley approached a group of individuals and held up her phone, showing them a picture of her and Curt at a party. They were smiling and pressed their cheeks together.

"Excuse me, have you seen this guy?" she asked, her voice slightly frantic. "He's our friend and we lost him on the way to the creek last night."

"I'm sorry, we haven't," they replied.

"Okay, thank you. If you do see him, please tell him to call Ashley or find us. We're camped up on the other side of the hill."

"Yes, we'll keep an eye out for him."

Ashley and her friends continued to approach anyone they could find, searching for Curt. They even ventured into a nearby cave, but he was nowhere to be found. Ashley expressed her frustration, stating that when Curt finally shows up, he better have a good explanation for his absence.

Feeling like she had no other choice, Ashley made the decision to run into town and ask around at the local diner and sheriff's office to see if anyone knew what happened to Curt. Her friends offered to go with her, but she insisted on going alone. She needed some time to herself as she searched for answers about Curt's disappearance.

As she walks towards the van, Ashley notices a girl standing in her path. The girl lowers her head and quickly glances up at Ashley as she passes by. Ashley takes in the girl's beautiful features: long black hair and stunning blue eyes, along with a lilac dress adorned with tiny orchid flowers. She is struck by the girl's beauty, but quickly remembers why she is here. "Excuse me, have you seen my friend Curt? I'm trying to find him," Ashley asks, showing the girl a picture of them together on her phone.

"Sorry, no I haven't," the girl replies before hurrying away and avoiding eye contact with Ashley. Not wanting to let her go so easily, Ashley stops her. "Wait a minute," she says. "Um, if I see him..."

The girl cuts Ashley off, "I'll let him know you're looking for him," the girl responds nervously.

"Thank you! By the way, what's your name?" Ashley asks.

"Tori. My name is Tori," the girl answers.

"Thanks Tori," Ashley says gratefully before continuing on her way.

The girl slowly averts her eyes and walks towards the right side of the path. Ashley turns to leave, but she hears Curt whisper her name. She quickly turns around, but he is nowhere to be found. The girl looks back at Ashley with pink glowing eyes before continuing down the path. Ashley is amazed by the unusual color of her eyes and catches herself with her mouth open in shock. 'What happened to her blue eyes? I've only seen that color in pictures or from red-eye flashes, but this is just creepy,' she thinks as she heads in the opposite direction.

Feeling like Tori is hiding something, Ashley walks up to the van and finds the spare key hidden in the fender. 'Yes, it's still here!'

She unlocks the door and starts the engine, driving down to the town of Beaver Creek and pulling up at the sheriff's office. Though she originally planned on asking about Curt, she now wants to report him as a missing person. As she reaches for her phone to call him one last time, she suddenly hears another phone ringing. Confused, she looks around and finds Curt's cell phone between the seats.

There are 18 missed calls, 2 voicemails, and 29 text messages waiting for him. 'He never took his phone!' Out of the calls, 13 are from Ashley, while both voicemails and 25 text messages are also hers. The rest are from a girl he dated at college a few months ago and three from his mom. Now feeling upset, Ashley grips the steering wheel tightly as she leans back into her seat. She then hits the wheel out of frustration, anger, and sadness over Curt's disappearance. Grabbing her purse and both phones, she walks into the sheriff's office.

"Hello, is there something I can help you with?" "Yes, sir. I need to report a missing person. What steps should I take?"

"First, I'll need some information from you. Can you tell me when and where this person was last seen?" Ashley tells Deputy Fred everything she knows, including her attempts to locate the missing person through questioning others, but with no luck. Deputy Fred asks for a description of the missing person and when Ashley last had contact with them. She shows him her phone, explaining that he never received her messages because he left it in his van. Deputy Fred suggests the possibility that he may have brought someone back to the van and dropped his phone during an intimate encounter.

"That could be possible," Ashley responds, "but he would have answered regardless. He always checks his phone and would have noticed my attempts to reach him."

Deputy Fred advises Ashley to return to the campsite with your friends and wait to see if the missing person to show up while he informs the sheriff's office and sends someone out to search the area. He also plans to contact the property owner to drive around and check if the missing person may be camping elsewhere nearby. Ashley agrees and leaves the office, hopeful but worried about her missing loved one."

Driving back towards the creek, Ashley spots the diner they had passed by last night. She pulls into the parking lot and makes her way inside.

"Howdy, have a seat wherever you'd like," yells Nell from behind the counter. Ashley takes a seat at the counter and browses through the menu. She ultimately decides to order six Beaver Creek special breakfasts which are supposedly "fit for a hungry beaver". The meal includes three eggs, bacon, ham, hash browns, biscuits with red eye gravy, grits, toast, and either two pancakes or French toast. "Wow, this is more like fit for a hungry bear," Ashley mumbles to herself.

Deputy Fred walks back to the Sheriff's office and knocks on the half-open door. He finds the Sheriff sitting at his desk reading the daily newspaper. Deputy Fred informs him that he needs to contact John Smith to see if he can take Hurley and his mule out to search for a missing kid. He explains what happened and gives a description of Curt. The Sheriff responds that he knew something like this would happen sooner or later with people falling into Devil's Attic. "If anything happens to this kid, there will be a mess on our hands - and on John's," the Sheriff remarks.

"Go ahead and call John," he instructs Deputy Fred. "But make sure he knows not to go down to the creek asking questions to anyone camping there. I'll join him shortly." The Sheriff adds that he doesn't want any fights or shootings over something said as it is John's property, and he has every right to ask people to leave."

Deputy Fred responds with a crisp "Yes, sir" before returning to the front of the office. He picks up the phone and dials John's number.

"Hey John, it's Deputy Fred. I'm doing well, how about you? Good to hear. The Sheriff wants me to ask if you can take the mule and Hurley out around the property to search for a missing young man. A girl came in earlier and reported that he's been missing since last night. And just a heads up, the Sheriff said not to go down to the creek and ask any questions about it. He'll be there soon to handle that. Thanks, John. Take care."

Arriving back at the parking area off the dirt road, Ashley grabs the boxes of food she bought at the diner. On her way down, she runs into Jeff and Holly who help her carry it the rest of the way.

"Wow, what a delicious breakfast spread," says Bryan too Ashley.

"Yeah, this food is amazing," adds Jeff.

"Thank you, Ashley. This is just what we all needed - some good food," says Holly gratefully.

"You're welcome," responds Ashley.

She proceeds to tell them about her trip into town and how she went to the Sheriff's office to file a report on Curt as a missing person. She also mentions that they are sending someone out to search and ask questions about him.

# 11

## "THE FIND"

John and Hurley hop on the mule and ride towards the old Stellar foundation, hoping to find a clean campsites. He doesn't want any litter blowing through the property.

As they weave through the trail by the field, the sun slowly rises above Sulfur Mountain, casting a golden light over the dew-covered grass and flowers. The sparkling droplets of water look like diamonds in the sunlight. The flowers turn their faces towards the sun, eagerly soaking up its vital energy. Throughout the day, they will track its movement across the sky, growing taller and stronger with each passing moment.

John takes in the beauty of nature and marvels at how the sun nourishes every living thing with its life-giving rays. The vibrant shades of green, the shimmering dew drops, and the stunning array of wildflowers all add to the breathtaking scenery around them. It's a peaceful and serene experience that fills John with wonder and gratitude.

"Good morning, everyone!" he calls out into the peaceful scene. He parks his mule and grabs his gear bag filled with essentials: garbage bags, hand shovel, bottled water, rope, flashlight, SD cards for his cameras, and a knife. As he heads down to the creek, he catches a whiff of smoldering fires in the air. Hopefully, whoever started them had enough sense to put them out, John thinks to himself. That's always his biggest concern.

He considered putting up warning signs around the creek, but he didn't want to attract more attention from thrill-seekers and partygoers looking for a place to cause chaos and leave a mess.

Hurley has already taken his morning swim and is now scouting the area to ensure it's safe for John to work. The loyal dog is also checking for any unauthorized visitors like rabbits and mice. John sets down his gear bag and takes in the sight before him with disbelief.

"Looks like there were a lot of people here this weekend, Hurley," he says with a shake of his head. "A bunch of kids by the looks of it. This is going to set us back on building the cabins for our employees' annual party in the fall." He sighs and realizes that he may need to hire some help to keep these unwelcome guests away on weekends if he wants to finish construction safely and on time.

John begins to pick up the litter scattered along the creek bank and the remnants of the old Stellar foundation. He hopes he has enough trash bags to collect it all. After three long hours, he finishes collecting the debris and extinguishing any remaining campfires with water. Loading the bags onto his mule, and then heads back to changes out the SD cards in the wildlife cameras he set up around the creek and cave, knowing there will likely be footage he doesn't want to see from unruly young adults having sex.

Luckily, he had hidden them in dummy bat boxes that have gone unnoticed so far. If he didn't they probably would steal or destroy them.

Once he completed resetting the cameras he decides to dig through the Stellar foundation. With his trusty hand shovel, John begins digging through the rubble of the old foundation, carefully sifting through every inch in search of any clues or remnants. Hours pass by as he diligently searches on his hands and knees, but eventually he sits back in defeat and remarks to Hurley, who is napping on the cool sand of the creek bank.

"Can you believe it? I found nothing, Hurley! Oh well, at least I brought us lunch today - corned beef sandwiches, coleslaw, and chips."

Hurley sits up and gazes at John. John stands up and walks over to the creek, using its water to wash his hands and clean off the shovel he had been using.

The sun is shining through the leaves of the trees above, creating a beautiful scene. As John takes in the surrounding nature eating his lunch with Hurley he can hear the soothing sound of a small waterfall down by the creek.

Birds are singing and bugs are chirping in the trees, blending with the earthy smell of the creek. Lulled by the peaceful atmosphere, John reflects on how pleasant it must have been to live here. He dips his hands into the cool water and notices rocks and little fish swimming nearby.

Suddenly, something catches his eye sticking out of the sand under the water. Curiosity piqued, he reaches down to feel it and runs his fingers along its smooth, rippled edges. It resembles one of those wooden instruments that you hold in your hand and rub with a wooden rod to make noise. As he continues tracing its edges, John slowly tries to lift it out of the sand. But then he realizes with a jolt that it's not an instrument - it's a human skull.

Gently, John pulls the object out of the water and sets it on dry land for a closer look. Piece by piece, he carefully unearths the different parts until he has reconstructed what appears to be a Native American warrior. The bones are still adorned with a chest plate made from bone. John shakes his head, wondering about the connection between Romanian and Native American cultures in this strange situation.

He knows he can't involve the authorities in this discovery; they would likely disturb the burial ground even further. So, he decides to dig a grave for the fallen warrior himself. He retrieves his shovel from the mule and finds a peaceful spot along the creek to lay him to rest. After digging a hole, John gently places each section of the warrior's remains into the grave before covering it with dirt.

As he finishes filling in the grave, John notices that the light filtering through the trees is starting to fade, as though a storm is approaching. But strangely, there are no signs of rain or thunder. Just as he stops to take in his surroundings, feeling the gentle breeze on his face, he realizes that this is no ordinary storm. It's something else entirely. He leans on his shovel and chuckles to himself, shaking his head as he gazes around at the woods and murmurs aloud, "Some things just aren't meant to be understood."

Knowing it is something supernatural as the hair on the back of his neck rises up. He figures he best speak to the spirits.

"My intentions are peaceful. I come to honor your fallen warrior and your people." The wind picks up, swirling around the speaker's legs and enveloping him in a tight coil. It spins him around, revealing a ghostly figure with an eagle head and glowing yellow eyes. Despite his fear, John is captivated by the being's beauty and feels a sense of peace emanating from it. "A'he'hee! A'he'hee!"

The figure communicates with John in a language he doesn't understand but can sense that it means no harm. As suddenly as it appeared, the figure vanishes into the wind, leaving John surrounded by calmness. The sun emerges from behind the trees, illuminating the creek again.

John finishes the topping of the grave disguises it with rocks and stones. He calls out his thanks to the mysterious being before carrying on with his day, feeling hungry after all the physical labor.

# 12

## "I REMEMBER NOW"

VICTOR ENTERS NELL's diner as the sun begins to rise over the mountains. The place is unusually crowded, and he wonders why as he sits at the counter facing the bustling kitchen. Nell, the owner, greets him and places today's newspaper in front of him with the main headline displayed. She quickly pours him a cup of coffee and asks if he wants his usual. Victor nods and takes a sip of the hot coffee, almost gagging when he reads the headline about a missing girl being found in a nearby cave.

He continues reading about the discovery of her body and an eerie finger bone in the old foundation on the property near the cave. According to the article, there are rumors that the area is cursed by demons and Skin-walkers who lurk at night looking for victims.

Victor lifts his head, observing Ed's frenzied movements in the busy kitchen. His youngest son scrambles to keep up with the mounting orders. As Victor watches the flames on the gas stove, the noise of the diner fades into the background. He becomes lost in thought, gazing into the dancing flames that remind him of a traumatic memory.

He remembers being tied to a log, surrounded by kindling and wood, as people shouted for him to be burned alive. The fire slowly crept up towards his body as he struggled to break free from the ropes binding him. He looks out at the crowd and sees his mother crying, dressed all in black. Suddenly, Nell's voice brings him back to reality.

"Victor? Are you okay?" she asks.

He assures her that he is fine and blames it on daydreaming. Nell laughs and teases him about finding a wild one last night that left a lasting impression on him. Victor playfully denies it, telling her that if he had found such a woman, he would still be in bed with her instead of working. They both laugh as Nell continues to serve customers and ring up orders.

He inquires Nell about her lack of assistance compared to Ed. She rolls her eyes and lets out a deep sigh, wishing she could find someone to help with the overwhelming workload. It's been this hectic for two days now. She says,

"You gave me an idea. I'll make a part-time help wanted sign and hang it in the window. Maybe someone will see it and be willing to work."

He asks if the recent influx of people is due to the newspaper article about the discovery of a dead girl's body. Nell confirms that most of their customers have been talking about it. People have been coming from all over, camping out on Beaver Creek and in the nearby caves, hoping to capture supernatural phenomena like demons, ghosts, and Skin-walkers on camera. Some are even searching for vampires and Moth man sightings have been reported based on internet rumors. Victor can't help but laugh at how far people will go for money.

Victor gets up and hands Nell the check with cash, "Keep the rest Nell you can give grumpy man a few dollars out of it if you want."

"I heard that Victor!" Ed yells out the window between the kitchen and the serving area.

"Thanks for the delicious breakfast Ed." Victor yells back.

Ed waves as Victor exits the diner.

Sitting in his car, Victor takes a moment to process everything that just happened at the diner.

"Am I going crazy?" he mutters to himself with a hint of disbelief.

He droops his head in his hands and massages his temples. The start of a migraine throbs at the base of his skull, causing him to slowly lift his head and run his hands through his hair. With stress weighing heavily on his mind, Victor comes to a realization and lets out a heavy sigh. He must obtain it, no matter the cost. And he knows John Smith has it. Reaching for the glove compartment in his car, he pulls out a bottle of ibuprofen to relieve the pounding headache. Without water, he tosses one into his mouth and swallows hard before starting his car and exiting Nell's parking lot.

# 13

## "THE ENCOUNTER"

THE VIBRANT COLORS of the setting sun behind Sulfur Mountain paint the sky with hues of orange, yellow, and pink. The flowers in the field turn to watch as the sun dips below the horizon. John unpacks his gear bag and takes before making Hurley some dinner.

He turns on his laptop and inserts an SD card from one of his wildlife cameras into the card reader. As he waits for the images to load, he pulls out a frozen baked ziti dinner from the freezer and sets it in the oven. He prepares Hurley's dinner, a mix of raw chicken, rice, organic kibble, and cottage cheese. Then, he heads for a quick shower before settling down at the computer.

With a cold Mike's Hard Lemonade in hand, John begins clicking through the images from the first SD card. "I hope there's something interesting on here," he mutters to himself.

"It's been pretty quiet out there lately."

He speculates that all the recent activity around the cave and creek may have disrupted things in the spirit realm. Clicking through photos of deer, turkeys, raccoons, and other typical visitors to his property, he suddenly comes across something unusual: a mist floating about two feet off the ground. He zooms in but sees nothing out of the ordinary.

He clicks to the next image and is startled to see four ghostly figures standing in a half circle formation. One stands just outside the group while another appears to be pointing or gesturing towards something behind them. Their whitish-blue bodies are almost transparent, giving them an eerie appearance.

John realizes that this is from the new camera he had set up facing a large walnut tree near the path leading down to the creek. He leans back in his chair as he thinks about what these spectral beings could be. Scrolling to the next image, he sees that the figures now have black slits for eyes. The one who was pointing is still gesturing, and its mouth appears to be open in a scream or shout, revealing a black void instead of teeth.

In the following photo, a ghostly figure seems to hang from the tree in the same spot where the three men were standing. John's heart races as he tries to make sense of these strange images.

He enlarges the image, but it becomes pixelated and hard to decipher. Is that figure in the distance George Stellar? Is he trying to communicate with me? Leaning back in his chair, he ponders this while studying the photo.

He gets up to tend to his dinner that's just finished cooking, John decides to load more images onto his computer and watch the local weather forecast.

Who is this ghostly apparition pointing at him and what are they trying to convey? Perhaps there's something significant about the large tree. I might need some assistance in researching all of this. It looks like it's time to start looking for a college student who is skilled in research.

Returning to his computer after dinner, John finishes going through the images on the first card. There are no more photos of the ghostly figure's. That's odd; they must have shown what they wanted to show.

Scrolling through the new images, his surprise grows. A girl emerges from the cave, her long black hair flowing and in a dress. It's strange that she didn't trip the camera on her way in. Perhaps she's with some other campers nearby.

He continues to browse through the images and realizes that there are people setting up campsites around the cave, starting fires, and enjoying drinks together. They seem to be behaving decently enough.

John counts at least fifteen different tents on both sides before reaching the end of the images. But he doesn't see the girl with the long black hair with any of them; perhaps she's camping higher up. Stretching his arms behind his head.

Exhausted from the events of the day, John finally goes to bed around midnight. As he drifts off to sleep, a dream takes hold of him. In his dream, a young girl appears wearing a beige dress or perhaps it's a nightgown. Her wet brown hair hangs in front of her face, making it difficult to see her features clearly. She stands in a creek, appearing almost white against the dark water. It's possible she is bathing in the creek, but something about her posture suggests shame. John tosses and turns in his sleep, eventually waking up on his right side facing the wall.

The camper is dark, with the curtains drawn to block out any light or potential peering eyes from outside. Despite this precaution, John can't shake the feeling that someone or something is watching him as he sleeps.

A sudden presence fills the room, and he can sense something standing beside his bed. Is he awake, or is this still a dream? He stays still for a few moments, trying to determine if he's truly awake. But as minutes pass by, he realizes that he is completely conscious and that there is truly something standing next to him.

Fear grips him, and his heart starts racing so loudly that it echoes in his head. Trying not to succumb to terror, John focuses on regulating his breathing. Inhale through the nose, exhale through the mouth. Slowly, his heart rate begins to slow down, and he gathers enough courage to slowly turn over and confront whatever or whoever is standing beside him. Please don't let it be that dark figure looming over me. With trembling hands, he turns over to see what is in the room with him.

He raises his arm with caution, sliding it behind him as if he were simply shifting in his sleep. Closing his eyes, he rolls onto his back and waits for a moment before slowly opening one eye, attempting to deceive whatever presence may be there. His vision is met with the shadow of a person standing next to him, about four feet tall or maybe slightly taller. He blinks a few times and realizes that it's a little girl with her head hanging down.

He jumps up in bed, gasping for air as he sees her pale skin. "Holy shit..." he mutters, realizing who she is. His eyes widen as he notices the deep slash marks covering her arms, like they were made by a large knife or sharp claws. Her nightgown is also torn and shredded in various places. He can't bring himself to look at her face, too afraid of what he might see.

"How...how are you real? This must be a dream," he stammers in disbelief.

He reaches out to touch the girl, hoping it's all just a figment of his imagination. But before his hand can make contact, she seizes his arm in a lightning-fast movement that leaves him stunned and unable to react. She moves with the same speed as the shifters who disappear like smoke. Her grip on his arm is strong and forceful, causing John to freeze up in fear. He tries to scream, but his mouth feels like it's been sealed shut. Tremors run through his body, causing the bed to shake along with him. He attempts to call out for help, but once again he is overcome with fear and cannot move.

The little girl's head tilts to the side, then to the other. It feels like a scene from a horror movie as he struggles to scream. Finally, he manages to let out a small cry that wakes up Hurley, who rushes into the room. Growling angrily, Hurley stands in the doorway and John knows he sees the girl too. Suddenly, she turns her face towards John, and he finally gets a good look at her.

Her face is cut just like her arms; her eyes are empty and black as a crows. There is an open gash on her throat with water trickling out of it. She seems like she's trying to speak, but can't because someone has slashed through her vocal cords.

Now even more terrified, John frees himself from her grip and leaps across the bed. The girl remains fixated on him before climbing onto the bed. Hurley's growls have now turned into deep barks, but soon return to grumbling growls.

John quickly jumps off the bed with Hurley right behind him. He rushes to the living room to grab his camera. He returns to the bedroom, eager to take a photo of her, but she has vanished. He frantically searches the small room and bathroom, but she is nowhere to be found. Hoping to capture her image on camera, he runs back to the living room and begins snapping photos inside the camper.

Frustrated and confused, he decides to check the time. It's 3:45 a.m., according to the clock in the kitchen. Exhausted both physically and mentally, he collapses onto the small couch, questioning what is real and what isn't the feeling of doubting himself. As he gazes up to the ceiling he slowly sinks down and drifts off to sleep.

# 14

## "KAI LIU"

THE CLOCK READS 2:45 a.m. in Falls Church, Virginia. The nurses on duty at Enova Fairfax Hospital are enjoying a quiet night on their floor. However, during full moons, they typically experience increased activity from some of their comatose patients, especially those under the influence of drugs. The medication seems to have less effect during the full moon, requiring higher dosages.

Dawn Phillips, a Registered Nurse that recently graduated nursing school is working the night shift, is completing paperwork at the nurse's station when she hears an alarm go off in room 612. She quickly gets up and rushes to the room, assuming it's just a sensor that has fallen loose or malfunctioned. Turning on the light, she checks on the patient.

"Everything looks normal here. What triggered your alarm?"

In her search for the culprit, Dawn's attention is drawn to Kai Moonfeather Liu, a young woman of American Indian and oriental descent in her mid-twenties. She watches as Kai attempts to lift her hand for the first time in weeks.

Two months prior, Kai had fallen into a coma and was brought to this hospital. Despite numerous tests, doctors are unable to determine the cause of her illness. The news of Kai's condition has spread throughout the FBI laboratory, prompting her boss Mr. Marcum to quarantine everything she is working on. Enova Fairfax Hospital was chosen for her medical care due to its larger size and advanced facilities.

Kai Liu is employed as a forensic lab technician, utilizing her bachelor's degree in Forensic Pathology to work on cases for the Beaver Creek, Kentucky sheriff's office. She was tasked with examining a human finger bone that still had a ring attached to it.

After conducting numerous tests and deciphering the message engraved inside the ring, she began to feel ill. Initially, she experienced chills and fever, followed by bouts of nausea, and eventually vomiting.

Her FBI colleagues at the Quantico laboratory found her sick in the women's bathroom one day and urged her to seek medical attention. She was hospitalized for a few days before slipping into a coma. Despite thorough testing, no known illness or bacteria could be identified as the cause of her illness.

Nurse Dawn watches Kai's hand move. Kai slowly closes her fingers into a fist and bends her arm at the elbow, raising it up. Then, she attempts to put her hand on her face. Nurse Dawn gently holds onto her hands and massages them in hopes of calming her down and preventing her from pulling out any IVs.

She calls for the charge nurse, Mrs. Meyer, who quickly rushes to Room 612. As Nurse Dawn tries to explain what happened, she speaks so quickly that Mrs. Meyer has to shake her to calm her down.

"Take deep breaths, Dawn. It's going to be okay. Kai must be trying to wake up; we need to contact the doctor right away. Do you understand? Please go out to the nurse's station and call the doctor immediately. Just try to stay calm, Dawn. Everything will be alright; she's just waking up."

Without hesitation, Dawn bolts from Room 612 and sprints to the nurses' station, snatching Kai's file along the way in search of her doctor. Meanwhile, Mrs. Meyer prepares the patient for her awakening. She adjusts the bed until Kai is sitting up at a 45-degree angle. Hurrying back to the room, Dawn joins Mrs. Meyer's side.

"Did you reach the doctor?"

"I couldn't; I got his answering service and left them an urgent message."

"That's okay, he should call back soon." The phone rings.. "Wait, that might be him now."

Mrs. Meyer answers the phone and informs Dr. Patrick that his patient is coming out of her coma. Dr. Patrick informs Nurse Dawn he'll be right up.

Rushing into Room 612, Dr. Patrick greets his recovering patient with a comforting smile and words of encouragement.

"Kai...can you hear my voice, Kai?" Dr. Patrick eagerly awaits a response from her. Kai slowly opens her eyes, blinking rapidly as if trying to extinguish a flame. Her eyes water and Nurse Dawn gently wipes away the tears.

"Hello, Kai. Do you understand me? I'm Dr. Patrick, I saw you a few months ago when you first came to us. How are you feeling? Can you tell me how many fingers am I holding up?"

Kai holds up three fingers.

"Great job Kai." Dr. Patrick says.

Trying to speak to Dr. Patrick, Kai struggles to form words as her throat is raw from the tube that was recently removed.

Understanding her difficulty, Dr. Patrick asks her to simply nod yes or no in response to his questions. She nods yes. He carefully explains the events that have occurred and encourages Kai to relax. As he speaks, her heart rate increases on the monitor beside them, reflecting the past few months she spent in a coma.

Nurse Dawn and one of the CNAs assist Dr. Patrick in preparing Kai for her next steps: eating on her own and learning to walk again. After being bedridden for so long, her muscles are weak and unable to support her weight. Finally, Kai musters enough strength to speak.

"Where is Mona?" she asks.

"Who is Mona, Kai?" Nurse Dawn inquires.

"My friend. She visits me all the time and talks to me every day," Kai replies.

"I'll have to check if Mona is on the approved visitors' list. If she is, I'll reach out to her for you. Now, let's focus on getting your strength back. Would you like some Jell-O?" Nurse Dawn offers. Kai nods in agreement.

After a few weeks, Kai has made a remarkable recovery and Dr. Patrick determines that she is well enough to return home. Despite not having any family in Virginia, she moved there from Arizona for college.

Finally, back at her apartment, Kai can start to piece her life back together. As she puts away her belongings and tidies up the space, she prepares a relaxing bath for herself. Using lavender bath salts and lighting candles around the tub, she sinks into the soothing warmth of the water. The tub is just big enough for her to fully stretch out and allow the salt-infused water to envelop her body. She drapes a hot cloth over her face, letting go of all tension and stress as she slips into a state of pure relaxation.

Who is Mona? The question echoes in her mind, repeating over and over. She can't seem to grasp the answer. How does she know this name? Where has she heard it before? All she sees in her mind is a woman standing in a black dress, but she can't make out her face; the woman seems sad. And then there's him - the man who comes to her in her thoughts. He's so vivid, she can almost feel his touch and smell his scent.

His presence brings her comfort and pleasure. But when she tries to visualize his face, all she can see is his long black hair and shapely lips. She's never kissed anyone as seductive as he appears to be. His unique scent envelopes her with desire, causing her body to tingle with anticipation. As she drifts into a trance-like state, she loses herself in fantasies of this mysterious man.

He feels so tangible, yet she is aware that they have never actually met. The longing for him intensifies, and she traces her hand along her neck as if he were caressing her. Her fingers glide down between her breasts, over her stomach, and finally to the place where butterflies flutter inside of her. She opens her eyes abruptly, realizing it's not his touch but her own.

"What is happening?" she mumbles as she pulls the towel off her face and sits up in the tub. Glancing at the clock on the wall, she sees that an hour and thirty minutes have passed since she entered the tub. She stands and dries herself, wrapping a towel around her body before walking out of the bathroom and collapsing onto her bed. Exhausted, she falls into a deep sleep.

The sound of the alarm pierces through the quiet stillness of Monday morning at 5:30 a.m. Kai groggily reaches over and hits the snooze button, but then remembers that she must work today. In a frenzy, she jumps out of bed and rushes to get ready.

As she walks into the FBI Laboratory, eager to start her day, she is taken aback by the sight in the employee's cafeteria. Her co-workers are all standing there, cheering and yelling. The room is decorated with banners that read "Welcome back, Kai" and there's a big cake and flowers waiting for her. She is greeted with hugs from all of her friends at the lab.

"Thank you, everybody, thank you so much. You really didn't have to do this."

"We missed you, Kai. Welcome back," her supervisor says warmly as he pats her on the back.

Even though she is excited, she can't help but feel a little embarrassed by all the attention focused on her. Being the center of attention has never been her preference; she sees herself as more of a loner. She feels like a bit of an outsider in this society, especially with her American Indian background which tends to be looked down upon by others. As much as she wants to escape the crowd and retreat to the lab, she puts on a smile and greets everyone with kindness.

Finally, up in the lab, she begins her work on new cases. She reminds herself to not overexert herself as per her supervisor's instructions. The cases assigned to her are not pressing matters. As she opens the file and sets out the evidence tray, she eagerly starts her testing.

Being back at work feels like a breath of fresh air; she is doing what she loves. She sets up the microscope and slides, ready to spend a few hours examining bacteria samples. Suddenly, she hears a faint voice calling out her name.

"Kai, my love, I miss you."

Startled, she jumps and accidentally knocks over a beaker of solution, causing it to shatter on the floor. Panicked, she looks around but sees no one else in the lab with her. Her fellow technicians hear the noise and look up from their own experiment stations. They work in separate glass areas but can still see their colleagues across the room. Pam, another technician, walks over to Kai to see if everything is okay.

"Are you okay, Kai?"

"Did someone come into this room?

"What do you mean? I haven't seen anyone else in your lab."

"Someone whispered in my ear just now."

"I haven't seen anyone coming or going. Are you sure you heard a voice?"

"I'm positive. It felt so real, I could feel their breath against my neck."

"Maybe you should take a break and make yourself some hot tea. It might help you relax."

"That's a good idea, Pam. Thank you."

Kai bends down to clean up the broken glass and spilled solution from the floor before heading to the break room.

Carrying her freshly brewed cup of tea, she heads back to her lab and passes by the quarantine evidence room. She feels a pull towards that room, as if something is calling out to her. Pausing for just a moment, she looks towards the door and senses a tingling sensation in her lower abdomen, like butterflies fluttering around. She can't help but feel an increasing desire for the man she dreams off. She catches a whiff of his familiar scent, but where is it coming from? Suddenly, her supervisor appears beside her and greets her. Trying to act surprised, she takes a gulp of her tea before responding.

"Hey there, Mr. Marcum! Just taking a quick break to grab some tea."

"How have you been feeling, Kai?"

"I'm doing well, thank you."

"Pam mentioned that something startled you in the lab?"

"Yes, I was completely engrossed in my work and I thought I heard someone call my name. It just caught me off guard."

"You don't have to push yourself too hard, you know. Take it easy on your first day back."

"Thank you for your concern, Mr. Marcum, but I feel good and ready to work."

As she enters her lab, she quickly takes a seat and begins to strategize. She knows she needs to sneak into the evidence room to retrieve something important, but she doesn't want anyone to notice.

After finishing her cup of tea, she glances around at the other scientists in their own labs, all engrossed in their work and not paying attention to her. Taking her cup with her, she confidently walks towards the evidence room and slides her key card through the lock to open the door. Just as she's about to enter, Mr. Marcum calls out to her. "Kai, what are you doing in there?"

"Just checking on something from my last case."

"You know you need permission from a supervisor, like myself, before entering this room."

"Oh right, I apologize Mr. Marcum."

"I'll let it slide this time, but next time you enter without asking first, I will have to document it and write you up. Understood?"

"Yes, sir, I understand."

Once she's inside, she explains to Mr. Marcum that she may have recalled something about the ring and needs to confirm her findings. She takes out the box and retrieves the file and bag containing the finger bone and ring. As she examines it, a sharp pain shoots through her side as if she's being stabbed with a knife. Her heart starts racing and she bends over in agony, clutching her side. Her supervisor asks if she's okay and she tells him its just menstrual cramps that will pass soon. He offers to get her some water, and she gratefully accepts.

As soon as Mr. Marcum leaves, the pain suddenly disappears. She clutches the evidence bag tightly, and this time she has a vision of a woman wearing a black dress watching someone being burned.

Shocked by the vividness of the vision, Kai grips the edge of the table with both hands and accidentally drops the evidence bag. In her mind, she sees the woman beckoning for her to follow into an open field of grass. Adrenaline surges through Kai's body, causing her to shake as if her blood sugar is dropping. Then, she catches a familiar scent in the air. It's a scent that makes her desires burn deep within her. She feels his strong arms wrap around her from behind, and she leans her head back onto his chest. He makes her feel safe and comfortable. Kai presses back against him, feeling every inch of his body pressed firmly against hers. His hands roam up her stomach, over both breasts, and squeeze them gently.

"Did you miss me? Did you miss my touch?" he whispers in her ear.

"Yes," she responds quietly, lost in the moment.

Mr. Marcum enters the room, he spots her clutching the edge of the table with both hands and tilting her head back. Concerned, he rushes over to her and offers her a bottle of water. She drops her head back, eyes and mouth wide open in shock. She realizes she was just reliving an intimate moment with the man from her memories, even though he is not physically present in the room with her. Her supervisor stands next to her, perplexed by her behavior.

"Oh my, these cramps are excruciating. I need to sit down," she says, trying to compose herself. He quickly pulls over a stool for her to sit on. She takes a few sips of water and holds onto her stomach as if in pain.

She tries to play it cool in front of her supervisor, but she can feel her cheeks burning with embarrassment. She trembles slightly as she explains that she just needs to take some ibuprofen for her cramps. Her supervisor allows her to leave and go home for a few hours. He tells her that she can come back if she feels up to it, or take the rest of the day off. It's entirely up to her.

At home on her couch, she clings to a pillow, trying to process what happened at work today. The memories of the man are becoming stronger and clearer in her mind. She knows now that he has something to do with the bone. She grabs her laptop and starts reading about Beaver Creek, Kentucky on Google.

Calculating the distance from her apartment to Beaver Creek, she finds that it's 558 miles away and would take approximately nine hours by car. "I could make that trip in half a day," she muses to herself.

Feeling excited about the possibility of visiting Beaver Creek, she asks her supervisor, Mr. Marcum, if she can have some more time off work. After checking her finances and realizing she has enough saved up, she decides to go ahead with the trip in the morning.

While researching American Indian visions on the computer, she comes across a wealth of information that resonates with her own experiences. She begins to understand why she has been having these feelings and visions of a woman. It dawns on her that she has a unique ability to see and feel things, as well as possessing knowledge that others may not have. She had never considered it a gift before, thinking instead that they were just random thoughts.

Eager to share her discovery, she calls her mother in Arizona and excitedly explains what she has found. Her mother reveals that this ability runs in their family but only in certain bloodlines within the tribe. She confesses that she knew this day would come when Kai would ask about her heritage. Her great-grandfather and grandfather were both medicine men and shapeshifters who used a combination of black and white magic: one for harm towards enemies and the other for healing the sick.

"I must warn you to be cautious and not reveal your true self," her mother cautions. "It is crucial to understand your abilities and how to control them. You can shift into different animals, so choose wisely if you prefer to stick with one form."

Most shapeshifters prefer to shift at night, but it is possible for them to do so at any time. A skilled shifter can do it with precision and go unnoticed by others. However, her mother warned her about the skin-walkers - dark magic users who can also shift their forms. They are not like regular shapeshifters; they use their ability to harm humans. They can even mimic the voices of loved ones or create sounds such as a crying baby to lure in their victims. Once someone gets close enough, they are torn apart and killed. Some of the creatures are inherently evil and should be avoided at all costs.

"Never make eye contact with them," Kai's mother warns her sternly. "They will sense that you are a shapeshifter and use that against you. You will feel their presence and hear their calls before you get close to them." Kai's mother stresses the importance of never looking these creatures in the eyes, no matter what happens, as it could cost her life.

After ending her phone call with her mom, Kai delves into researching shapeshifters in Native American tribes. She is fascinated by how they transform, what it feels like, and the abilities they possess. With eager anticipation, she begins searching for more information on the computer.

According to what she reads, shapeshifting brings a sense of freedom and allows one to seamlessly take on another form. Some shifters can change at will while others have more control and always remain in their human form. They also have remarkable healing powers and can heal faster than humans. However, it takes skill and practice to mimic someone else's appearance and this ability drains them if used too frequently. Before shifting, they may notice small changes in their body such as a change in hair color or heightened senses.

The next morning, Kai is excited about the making the trip. After loading her car with her luggage she sets off for Beaver Creek.

# 15

## "THE CORPSE"

JOHN TAKES the mule and Hurley out to roam along the tree line that marks the border between the field and Beaver Creek. Hurley eagerly runs ahead, trying to flush out birds and chase rabbits, while John follows on the mule behind.

The morning is perfect, with beautiful flowers dotting the field and a clear blue sky above. As they slowly make their way through the lush grass, John can't help but appreciate the peacefulness of this spring day.

As he reaches the end of the field and scans the area, John realizes that Hurley is nowhere to be seen. He searches through the field and among the trees, but there's no sign of him.

"I hope he didn't wander off to the creek and bother those campers," John mutters.

Suddenly, he hears Hurley's loud barks. Turning his mule around, John heads towards the source of the noise.

When he arrives, Hurley is excitedly jumping on his hind legs and spinning in circles as if he's found something special. John approaches, Hurley takes off running towards the tree line and the edge of the field. When John catches up, Hurley lies down and shows him what he found.

John turns to Hurley and speaks in hushed tones, "What the hell could it be?" Hurley takes a few steps closer, squinting at the object laying on the ground.

"Looks like a person's body. How long do you think they've been here?" John cautions Hurley to stay back as he slowly circles around the body, taking in every detail. He notices a dried flower clutched in the hand of the deceased. "A chicory flower," he observes. Keeping his distance, John examines the flower closely without touching either it or the body. He knows better than to disturb a potential crime scene.

John immediately calls the sheriff and relays what he has found. The sheriff says he will be arriving at John's shortly to investigate further.

He quickly rushes back towards the sheriff, who is waiting by the camper. The sheriff jump's into the mule and they drive back to where the body lies.

Upon closer inspection, John reveals that he believes it's not a recent death. As they approach the body, the sheriff warns John to be careful where he steps; this could potentially be a crime scene. John dismisses his concerns, stating that it's clearly an old carcass. But the sheriff notices something peculiar about the body and points to its head with a pen.

"It looks like someone has smashed it like a watermelon, and there is a hole in the neck." He speculates that whatever happened must have sucked out all the brains through either the mouth or neck. The body is so desiccated that it's difficult to determine its true age. The sheriff uses his pen to pry open the mouth and discovers yet another anomaly.

"I can't believe the jaw and mouth area are in one piece. Do you see this, John?"

"Yes, what is it?"

"These are invisible braces, a relatively new development in dental technology. This body is not old."

Looking down at the back of the body, he notices two small holes. "What are those?" John asks,

"I'm not sure. We'll have to call the forensic team back out here. Unfortunately, I have a feeling that this might be the missing young man we've been searching for."

John chuckles, "There's no way that's a 21-year-old laying there, Sheriff."

"I know, but I have a gut feeling about it and those usually turn out to be right."

John kneels to get a better look at the corpse. As he gazes upon it, he can't help but think, "Such a tragic fate; this poor soul must have endured a terrible ordeal."

On their way back to the camper, the sheriff decides that he wants to interview the people gathered at the creek. He instructs John to remain silent and stand behind him while he speaks to them. The sheriff plans on asking everyone to leave, citing that it is now a crime scene, and anyone who refuses will receive a trespass ticket and must appear in court with accompanying fines.

The sheriff approaches the group and informs them that he has some questions regarding a missing young man. He asks if anyone has seen Curt, describing his appearance. The sheriff then reveals that this area is now considered a crime scene but refrains from sharing too many details in order to prevent upsetting Curt's friends.

Immediately, the group begins packing up and leaving. The sheriff then pulls Ashley and her friends aside for further questioning about Curt, asking if there is anything they may have forgotten to mention before to him or Deputy Fred, such as any identifying features like a watch or dental work.

Ashley speaks up and mentions that Curt had recently gotten invisible braces put on about 7 months ago. After hearing this detail, the sheriff realizes it must be Curt's body found in the field. John hangs his head in disbelief, trying to understand how the young man ended up lifeless in his field.

The sheriff instructs everyone to leave the area and Ashley starts crying. She asks how Curt will get home if they leave, to which the sheriff assures her that he will call her when they find him. However, she explains that they all live three hours away. The sheriff advises them to go home for now until they can locate Curt and have an identified the remains found in the field.

The sheriff leads John up the hill and stops to ask if they are on the same page.

"Are you thinking what I'm thinking?" he asks.

"That the body is Curt's?"

"Yep, my hunch was right," the sheriff confirms.

They hear Ashley's voice calling out to them. They both turn towards the edge of the creek where she stands.

"Did you talk to that girl, Tori?" Ashley inquires.

"Tori? I haven't come across anyone by that name. What does she look like?" the sheriff responds.

Ashley tells him that she saw a girl on the path leading to the van. She seems distant and guarded, as if she knows something she doesn't want to share.

"She said her name was Tori."

John interrupts to add, "Long black hair, mini dress?"

"Yes, that's her," Ashley confirms.

The sheriff asks how John knows this and he explains that he has seen Tori before leaving the cave. He even has footage from one of the cameras facing the entrance. When asked, John says he can pull up the picture on his laptop. Without another word, they all walk away. On their way back to the camper, the sheriff requests to see the photo.

# 16

## "THE CAVE"

Back at the camper John asks the sheriff if he knows what A'he'he A'he'he means.

"It does sound familiar," he says.

"Sounds like Cherokee. Why do you ask John?"

"I heard it in the woods, I know sounds crazy but it was in the wind when I was down by the old stellar place."

"Interesting to say the least. Lot of strange things lately out in these woods."

"Yes sir sheriff and I have some more images to show you if you'd like to take a look?"

John brings up images on his laptop and sifts through them, pointing out some of the more recent additions.

"Hold up, let's go back for a minute." The sheriff requests.

He pauses at one image in particular, showing three ghostly figures standing in a semi-circle while another stands farther away.

"That is unsettling..." The sheriff observes.

"Yeah, it is. And look at this one. He seems to be pointing at something while they all face the camera." At the sheriff's request, John zooms in on the image.

"Is that your porch light in the background?"

"No the camera is facing away from the camper. It's actually facing the old walnut tree and the trail to the creek."

The sheriff let out a low whistle. "That's spooky..." he commented, staring at the photograph.

"Yeah, it sure is," I agreed, pointing to a figure in the picture.

"Look at this one. He's pointing at something and the others are looking right at the camera."

"Do you see that light? It looks like a lantern on a porch. You can even see the flame." The sheriff observed.

"That must be the old Stellar homestead, and that man must be George Stellar."

"I thought it was just a lightning bug in the background, I never thought it could be a lantern. That's eerie!" John replies.

"It's like you had somehow captured a moment from another era on camera. It was truly surreal and unnerving." The sheriff says.

"What do you think they are sheriff?"

"I have no clue. I've never encountered anything like this," the sheriff replies.

They decide to create a map of the area to determine where the mysterious figure is pointing, hoping to decipher its message.

John decides to tell the sheriff about his dream involving a ghostly young girl who appeared in his bedroom and attempted to climb onto his bed.

"According to legend, Anne and George Stellar had two daughters. Supposedly, they were on their way to church when they were stopped by the Marshal and his men. The men assaulted and tortured the girls, and the youngest one was tragically killed when they tied rocks to her and threw her into the creek."

"I always thought it was just a story, but there might be some truth to it," the sheriff confesses.

John explains that he is meeting with a girl to potentially hire her as a research assistant, and they hope to uncover the truth soon.

After clicking through various images, they finally come across a picture of a girl wearing a light-colored dress with black hair and lilac flowers.

The sheriff remarks, "I bet those are the footprints we found in the cave. She must have been barefoot."

"I think you're right," John agrees.

Hurley starts barking and John gets up and looks out the window.

Just then, CSI technicians arrive, and the two men lead them back to the corpse.

After about an hour of searching and taking photos of the body and area the CSI technicians leave.

"We need to explore this further, so let's head down and see what we can find," the sheriff tells John.

John grabs some flashlights from the mule, and they venture into the cave. After walking a few hundred feet, John notices fresh footprints leading deeper into the cave. The sheriff confirms they are recent, and they decide to follow them to see where they lead. They assume it must be the same girl who has been missing, and they want to find out what she could be doing in the cave.

They squeeze through tight spaces and finally enter a large room with a musty, earthy smell lingering in the air. The sheriff shines his flashlight around and notices a granite slab in a small hollowed-out area, like a hidden room within the larger one.

As he explores further, he comes across symbols and writings on the walls which he identifies as a combination of witchcraft and Native American symbols. It dawns on him that this may have been used as a sacrificial or ritual chamber to raise the dead. He also finds herbs mixed with mud and feathers, along with smudge sticks burning behind the table. Clearly, someone has been performing rituals here.

"This chamber was likely used by a witch or warlock, possibly even a necromancer. Its age is uncertain. Did you know that Anne Stellar, who was accused of witchcraft, was burned at the stake here?" The sheriff says, and John nods in agreement.

They both follow the footprints deeper into the cave until they reach a large body of water. The footprints seem to lead straight into the water. Using their flashlights, they scan around the edges and notice massive rock formations resembling columns, with curtains of stone hanging above them adorned with stalactites. In one area, they spot a glittering surface of white crystals. The sheriff identifies it as gypsum rock, a type of mineral.

John crouches down and shines his light beneath the water's surface, searching for any signs of movement or objects. They see several small springs bubbling up from the bottom. The sheriff informs John that it is probably pure mineral water, potentially artisanal. He adds that it is excellent drinking water and has health benefits.

Curious, John cups some of the water in his hand and brings it up to his nose before taking a sip. He notes that it has no unpleasant smell and tastes clean and refreshing.

"Wow, this mineral water is like nothing I've ever tasted before. It almost has a hint of lemon in it."

"Like the waters at Big Rock Candy Mountain in Utah?" the sheriff asks.

"Exactly like that." They both share a laugh.

Suddenly, they hear a noise coming from across the cavernous room. They quickly shine the flashlights in that direction, catching a glimpse of something grayish white darting into the darkness.

"Where did it go?" They both jump and scan the area with their flashlights.

John believes it went into a hole in the wall. They cautiously make their way over to investigate. John lets the sheriff take the lead, keeping his firearm at the ready just in case.

"I wonder what that was. I have an image of something similar on my computer."

"I remember. You showed me some media footage back at the office. Maybe we should set up some cameras down here, John."

"That's a great idea," John replies.

"I'll help you with that. I might be able to get them approved as part of our budget for investigative equipment. I'm curious to see what else is going on down here."

The two of them point there flashlights towards the hole, which is about four feet tall and five feet wide. After noticing that it continues deep into the cave, John suggests they crawl through and follow it. The sheriff reminds him that they are already far into the cave and nobody knows they're there. He thinks chasing after a mysterious creature in the darkness is not a wise decision.

John agrees with him and they make their way back across the room. They discuss setting up more cameras and using stronger lights for their next visit.

Suddenly, they hear a high-pitched noise followed by a low growl. Then, they catch snippets of conversation in what sounds like a fast-paced foreign language. They speculate that it might be Latin. Both are afraid but don't want to admit it to each other. Instead, they stand their ground and try to act unfazed by the eerie noises surrounding them.

The cave is filled with the light from their flashlights, casting shadows everywhere as they search back and forth. Suddenly, another voice echoes through the cave.

This time, it says "Stay away! Stay away from here!"

"Did you hear that, John?"

"Yes, I did. And I have a feeling that wasn't a polite request. It sounded more like a warning."

"If we keep on going, whatever it is might attack us." Sheriff Taylor's grip tightens on his gun as he agrees to leave the cave immediately.

When they turn to leave, there's a thump behind them that makes both of them jump and spin around. Heartbeat's racing, the sheriff raises his gun and shines his flashlight towards the source of the noise. They see a grey creature with fiery red eyes, long bony fingers with sharp claws, and teeth like fangs bared at them. Its skin is slimy and hairless, standing hunched over like an old man who can barely walk.

The sheriff warns the creature, "Don't come any closer or I'll have to shoot!"

The creature seems to understand and stops advancing towards them, taking a few steps back. The sheriff explains that they mean no harm and are simply looking for someone. John speaks up, asking what the creature is and what it wants. The creature tilts its head in thought before baring its teeth like an animal and growling, warning them to stay away. It leaps away into the darkness as they shine their lights around, trying to track its movement.

The sheriff spots the creature and calls out a name, "Benny, Benny Saxon!"

The creature, now climbing up a wall, turns its head in response to the call. It's face shows a mix of surprise and confusion, as if it recognizes the name. Without hesitation, it takes off into the darkness with such speed that they struggle to keep their lights on it.

"I think we should leave now!" Sheriff Taylor says.

They emerge from the cave at full speed, breathing heavily as if they just ran for miles. Trying to make sense of what just happened, they exchange a glance and speak simultaneously. They stop and John tells the sheriff to continue.

"I called out to the creature, and it seemed to understand me. I said Benny Saxon's name."

"I heard you. Do you really think it's possible that he is Benny Saxon?"

"It's possible! Maybe somehow, he survived the fall and this creature helped him survive. Or perhaps he became a creature himself, living in the caves. He was young when he disappeared in the 1960s, so he could have learned from the cave creatures and adapted to their ways. The fall may have caused brain injuries that prevented him from leaving to find his family."

"That's a valid theory, Sheriff. But what about the girl going into it?"

"I'm not sure about that. Maybe she enters the water for healing or as a fountain of youth. Perhaps it's like a spring of longevity." He chuckles.

"The fountain of youth."

Wouldn't that be something?" John laughs along with him as they make their way back up the hill to the mule.

# 17

## "ELLIE"

"GOOD AFTERNOON, my name is Ellie Owens. I saw your advertisement for a research assistant, and I'm interested in the job."

"Hello there, Ellie. My name is John Smith, and I am indeed seeking a research assistant to aid in investigating the history of my property. Specifically, I need help with tracing family lineages in the Beaver Creek area."

"That sounds like an intriguing project. I have strong research skills, as I am currently studying to become a paralegal assistant. I'm pursuing my degree online."

"Well, it seems you have the necessary qualifications. The position is part-time, but if there is an influx of information, we can discuss adjusting your hours. I understand that you are also attending school."

"Yes, that would be perfect for me. When could I start?"

"If this sounds agreeable to you, why don't we meet at Nell's Diner in town in about an hour to further discuss the details?"

"That works for me, sir. I will see you in an hour."

John pulls into Nell's Diner and finds a booth. He orders two glasses of water and asks Nell if she knows Ellie Owens. She confirms that she does and promises to direct her to John when she arrives.

"Hi Ellie, come with me John is over here in a booth waiting for you." Nell takes Ellie to where John is sitting.

Ellie joins John in the booth and takes out her notebook and pen, ready to take notes on their meeting. As John explains his research project and what he expects from her as his research assistant, Ellie listens intently. He mentions the pay rate of $15 per hour plus reimbursement for any expenses, which he assures her he will cover. Then he goes into detail about the property he purchased and the strange events occurring there. He fears it may scare her away, but Ellie reveals that she was born and raised in the area and is already familiar with the situation from local college and high school students, as well as the buzz on social media about the Beaver Creek murders and missing girls. She also adds that the rumored ghosts in the woods have gone viral on the internet.

Surprised by this new information, John leans back in his seat before responding.

"I had no idea it had gained so much attention."

She informs him that she has connections with many of the townspeople, especially the elderly who may remember the Saxons and the history of the Stellar homestead. John is particularly interested in learning about George Stellar and his daughters. What really happened to them? Ellie reveals that her grandparents used to tell stories about the old Stellar farm, which she was raised to believe were just campfire tales.

"I will get you a iPad and a laptop for you so you can conduct your interviews." John says.

"If you have anything else you'd like me to get please let me know."

"I do have a list if you don't mind getting these few things for me I'd really appreciate it sir."

She provides him with a list, and they exchange contact information. Excited to get started, Ellie heads to the local library to dig up information on the homestead. Meanwhile, John travels to Somerset to acquire the items Ellie requested. When he returns to Beaver Creek, he notices that Ellie is still at the library. He pulls into the parking lot and brings her the bag of supplies.

"Excuse me, Mr. Smith. Why do you have both an iPad and a laptop?"

"I realized it would be difficult for you to lug around a laptop while visiting people's homes and trying to type everything they say. So, I got you an iPad mini because it has a voice recorder, video camera, and regular camera. You can record conversations and take videos, then transfer them to your laptop later."

"That's perfect! Thank you so much."

Ellie shares her findings from the microfiche film of old newspapers from 1966. According to the article she reads, one of the Saxon children fell down a hole that turned out to be a deep cave on their property. While they are discussing this, Janice, the librarian, walks by and notices what they are looking at on the microfiche. The headline reads "Benny Saxon Missing in Large Cave."

Curious, she asks John why they are researching this information. He explains their investigation to her. Janice reveals that she remembers everything about the incident.

"I knew Martha Saxon. She was friends with my mother and me."

John asks if she can provide any information or insights. Janice leads them into a separate room where they can work without being disturbing by other library patrons.

In this room, they have access to all necessary resources such as reference books, computers, copiers, and fax machines.

"On that day, Benjamin was working in the coal mine down the road while Martha stayed home with their kids, Benny Jr., and Christopher. The boys were out hunting for deer to stock-pile winter meat but instead stumbled upon a large hole they believed to be a well. Benny, being the eldest and more knowl-edgeable, measured the depth of the hole by dropping rocks into it and counting as they fell. Little did he know the actual depth was a lot deeper than he figured. Excited to explore this mysterious cave, the boys snuck into their father's barn to gather supplies: an old miner's hat and plenty of rope. After tying the rope together, they returned to the cave.Benny anchored himself to the nearest tree while Chris slowly fed him down the hole. As he descended, he could hear water dripping and feel that the rock was wet. He also noticed that the space opened into a large area. Chris kept talking to his brother until he suddenly heard Benny scream and saw the rope start to pull back up. It tugged so fiercely that it almost pulled Chris down with it, but he let go just in time and stopped at the edge of the hole. Looking down, he could see the light from Benny's miner's hat swinging wildly as if some-thing had grabbed hold of him and was tossing him around. In a panic, Chris screamed for his brother and tried to grab onto the rope to pull him back up but, as he grasped the rope once more, Chris was jolted violently from side to side, his brother's screams ringing in his ears. When he finally reached the end of the rope and pulled it up, there was no weight on the other end. It hung limp and lifeless, covered in blood. In a panic, Chris ran back to the house, bursting through the kitchen door where his mother Martha and sisters were preparing vegetables for canning. Between sobs, Chris managed to tell them what had happened. But Martha couldn't understand him, so she took hold of him and told him to calm down and start over. After realizing what had happened, Martha grabbed Chris and they raced across the field to the ridge where the cave was located. There, they saw the bloody rope lying on the ground and Martha cried out, dropping to her knees in shock and grief."

"Oh my that's terrible." John expresses.

"Martha shouted into the depths of the mine, hoping for a response from her son Benny, but all she received was an eerie echo. She rushed back to the house to get help, first calling her husband's workplace to relay the news, and then phoning Sheriff Carl Taylor for assistance."

John interjects, asking if it is the same sheriff who is currently in office. Janice clarifies that it was his father who responded to the call for help.

She continues with her story, explaining how Sheriff Taylor arrived at the Saxon house with Benjamin, Martha's husband.

"Benjamin quickly gathered his harness and rope and had Chris guide them to the cave where Benny went missing. With his mining cap on and light shining, Benjamin descended 75 feet into the cave. He noticed ledges of rocks jutting out along the walls as far as his light could reach. As he stood on one ledge, he saw a piece of shirt stained with blood - undoubtedly belonging to his son. Overcome with grief, he sobbed and called out Benny's name, only to hear his own desperate cries echoing back at him, making him realize just how vast and daunting this cave was. Slowly descending to the ledge fifteen feet down, he scanned his surroundings and saw an opening in the cave wall on the other side. It was too far for him to reach, and he had no equipment to climb the sheer wall. The opening seemed big enough for someone to enter or exit. He prayed that Benny had landed on the closer ledge and climbed up to the opening, finding a way out. Benjamin crouched down and laid his hand on the rock, praying for his son's safety. As he lifted his hand, he noticed it was covered in something slimy and gooey. He wiped it off on his pants and called out for Benny again, realizing that he may never have made it to the opening. He must have fallen deeper into the cave, lost forever. Tears streaming down his face, Benjamin tugged on the rope for help out of the cave."

"Wow that is so sad what happened."

"Yeah it was and the he sheriff declared Benny missing for two years before finally filing it as an accidental death when there were still no signs of him. To honor their lost son, the Saxon family planted a maple tree near the cave, known for producing the sweetest and most delicious sap in the county. Every year, Martha would turn this sap into syrup and sell it to a local diner, using the proceeds to continue searching for her son and supporting her family financially. As time passed, Benjamin Sr.'s health declined due to black lung disease from working in the mine, and he passed away three years after Benny's disappearance. This took a toll on poor Martha, but Martha remained strong to hold their family together despite her own grief. She found purpose in taking care of their four remaining children and shared that it was what kept her going every day.

"I'll have to tap that tree again and make syrup in honor of Benny Jr.," John says firmly.

"That would be wonderful, Mr. Smith," Janice replies.

"Do you happen to know anyone else who might have information on the Stellar family?" John asks.

"Yes, let me go grab my address book from my office. I'll be right back."

After a few minutes, Janice returns with a piece of paper containing several names.

"Here, Mr. Smith, these are some people I believe can help you," she says as she hands him the list. John passes it too Ellie.

"Thank you again, Janice," he says gratefully.

"You're welcome. Glad I could be of assistance," Janice responds with a smile.

John and Ellie gather their notes and leave the library. Once outside, John expresses his surprise at how much they were able to uncover, and Ellie promises to contact the people on the list tomorrow. She also plans to transfer her notes onto their new laptop.

# 18

## "BEAVER CREEK MOTEL"

Kai Moonfeather Liu arrives at the Beaver Creek Motel, located on North Main Street in Beaver Creek, Kentucky. It's close to 6 p.m. on a Tuesday evening, and the parking lot is mostly empty with only a few cars scattered around. The motel is a quaint family-owned business with 21 rooms and a newly renovated exterior. The brown brick building is accented with white trim and Victorian details on the doors and walkway, stretching from the main lobby to Room 21. Each room has its own designated parking spot in front, and there are convenient amenities for guests such as laundry facilities, an ice machine, and vending machines for snacks and drinks centrally located between rooms 10 and 11.

With her purse in hand, she enters the lobby and approaches the front desk to inquire about room availability. The night clerk greets her and asks if she needs a room. Kai requests a single non-smoking room for a week, and upon seeing her FBI badge, the clerk offers a 25% discount for government employees. She then asks if Kai is here to investigate the corpse found on Sulfur Mountain. Kai gives her a strange look but plays along, confirming that she is indeed here for that reason.

The clerk hands Kai the key to Room 12 and informs her that it comes with free HBO & Showtime as well as other cable channels. Kai takes the key and parks her car in front of the door. As she unloads her luggage, she gets an uneasy feeling. Ignoring it, she opens the trunk and gazes at the three bags lying on the black carpet. Suddenly, she feels dizzy and closes her eyes for a moment. A vision flashes through her mind of a man sitting on a stool, but everything else is blurry except for him. He has shoulder-length hair and is wearing a dress shirt and tie. He slowly turns around and looks over his shoulder, sensing her presence. Overwhelmed by the vision, Kai falls to the ground in shock.

The connection is broken, and the vision fades away. But before she disconnects, she captures a clear image of his face in her mind. Those eyes, mesmerizing hazel orbs with a hint of greenish-yellow radiating from the center around his pupils. She knows those eyes. He was staring intently at her, as if he could see through her soul. Suddenly, a woman approaches Kai from across the parking lot.

"Are you okay?" she asks with concern.

"Oh, yes, I'm fine. I just tripped over my bags," Kai replies, realizing that during the vision she must have taken her bags out of the car and placed them on the ground next to her without realizing it.

"I saw you fall and thought something was wrong. But I didn't notice your bags there when you fell...that's odd."

"No, I'm fine. Thank you for checking on me."

"You're welcome." The kind stranger takes Kai's hand and helps her up.

She unlocks the door of her room and the smell of a motel room floods her senses. Throwing her bags on the chair and table next to the window she opens her toiletry bag and grabbing a can of disinfectant spray Kai sprays the room and all the bedding.

"Wow that is a bit better."

Kai collapses onto the edge of her bed, feeling exhausted yet hyperaware. She senses his presence strongly and knows he must be here.

Laying on the bed with her eyes closed, thinking of him and his unique scent, she realizes that her powers are developing rapidly. Though she's not entirely sure what she is, her mother warned her to be aware of changes and to always keep her surroundings in mind. Whenever she feels strange or experiences a sudden shift or vision, she wants to be alone – no normal people around to judge or try to lock her away for testing.

Kai gets up and turns on the air conditioning. She pulls the curtains shut for privacy before undressing. While walking towards the shower to turn it on, she catches a glimpse of herself in the mirror and takes out her ponytail holder. But as she looks at herself more closely, something seems off. Her eyes are changing color. She leans closer to the mirror and opens her eyelids wide in shock. Instead of their usual dark brown, one eye is now a vibrant emerald green with a yellow glow around the pupil while the other is a mix of purple and blue with the same yellow glow. Taking a step back from the mirror, Kai stares at herself in disbelief at this new development.

What is that?" She exclaims, reaching for her phone to call her mother.

"Mom, something weird is happening to my eyes. What should I do?" She panics.

Her mother explains that she is developing powers and will experience physical changes, some of which may be permanent. The different colors in her eyes will signify her tribe.

"Do you remember your great grandpa and grandpa Red Bear?" her mother asks.

"Of course," Kai replies.

Her mother tells her that their eyes were half-colored and sometimes all one color, with green or blue spots. "That's a trademark of our tribe."

Kai asks how she can prevent the changes from happening. She doesn't want to transform into something unexpected while she's in Beaver Creek, Kentucky or end up in the hospital because of a powerful vision.

"Don't be afraid, dear. It's not as scary as it seems. No matter what you do, it's going to happen. Just make sure you're in a safe place when it does. It won't stop, so find shelter and wait for it to pass, which could take anywhere from a few minutes to a few days," Kai's mother assures her.

After hanging up the phone, Kai feels a surge of panic and begins to feel light-headed again. She gulps down a glass of water and lies down on her bed for a little while. When she stands back up, she suddenly passes out and falls onto the bed.

She jolts awake at the sound of loud banging on her door. It sounds like someone is using a sledgehammer to try and break through. Kai quickly grabs her robe and goes to see who it is. Peering through the peephole, she sees the hotel maid standing outside.

Kai can't understand why the maid would be here so late at night. She opens the door and asks with confusion in her voice, "Room service?" feeling uncertain if this is all just a strange dream.

"Unfortunately, we don't offer room service," the maid replies apologetically.

"I'm the maid do you require your room cleaned today ma'am?"

"Hmm I don't think so, I just arrived about an hour ago."

The clerk looks at her list.

"Here it says you checked in at 6:18pm yesterday evening."

Kai scratches her head confused.

"Ma'am do you require your room cleaned or need fresh towels?"

"No I don't need my room cleaned, but I will take a couple of towels."

"You have a good day ma'am. If you require any other services to your room you need to contact the front desk before 3 PM today."

Kai nods in understanding and thanks the maid before closing the door to her hotel room.

She walks over to the window and pulls back the curtains slightly, squinting at the bright sunlight outside. It can't be morning already, she thinks, rubbing the back of her head. Did I really sleep for that long? She checks the clock on the night-stand and sees that it's 10:15 am. "Oh wow, I slept for over 12 hours!" she exclaims to herself. Feeling groggy from her long nap, she decides to take a hot shower to wake up. As she gets dressed, she notices a flyer for a local diner on the table and decides to check it out for breakfast. She hasn't eaten since yesterday afternoon while driving to Beaver Creek from Virginia on Interstate 75.

"I need to find some food I'm starving. I'll go check the front desk and see if there is anything good in town."

Kai walks out of her room and gets in her car. Pulling up to the front of the motel she gets out and goes in looking at the brochures of the local business.

"Can I help you with something ma'am?" A male voice calls out.

"Hi I'm looking for a good place for breakfast?"

"Oh, that would be Nell's diner in town."

"Ok, how do I get there?"

"Pull out of the motel and make a left follow it all the way down about a mile or mile and half and you'll see the sign and the restaurant."

"Thank you."

The diner, called Nell's, seems like a good option. She gets in her car and pulls out on to the road. Driving slow she finally sees the red sign on the right.

Kai parks and heads into Nell's Diner, noticing that it is incredibly busy. She realizes that it would be better to just take her order back to the motel room. As she approaches the counter, Nell greets her with a warm smile and hands her a menu.

Kai takes a seat on one of the bar stools and peruses the options. Suddenly, she feels butterflies in her stomach, causing her to wonder why this is happening again. In a diner of all places! Then, she feels a jolt on her shoulder and realizes that she had accidentally bumped into the man sitting next to her. She turns to apologize and is met with his smiling gaze. She is completely captivated by his eyes, his touch, and his scent. It's him, she thinks to herself in excitement and apprehension. She can't look away from his penetrating gaze as he seems to see right through her.

Nell interrupts their moment by asking if Kai is ready to order, but she doesn't hear her at all. She is to lost in the man next to her. He breaks her train of thought by reaching up and grabbing her hand.

"I'm sorry, I didn't hear you," Kai says as she finally tears her gaze away from him.

She quickly tells Nell her order - a turkey club with mayo on the side, coleslaw, baked chips if they have any, and a green tea with honey and lemon - all to go.

"Thanks!"

Kai lowers her head, stealing a glance at the man next to her. He's not looking back, but she can still catch his scent. It's intoxicating to her. She inhales deeply through her nose, trying to absorb every bit of his fragrance. It has a soothing effect on her, calming her nerves and making her feel almost drugged. She never expected to find him here, but she did.

That was her sole purpose for coming here. With a sudden urge, Kai stands up and makes her way to the women's bathroom.

Walking through the door of the bathroom and towards the sink, the tingling sensation returns, stronger than before. She has to hold onto the sink to keep herself from falling over. It's like he's inside her, awakening something deep within that brings immense pleasure. Standing in front of the mirror with her hands gripping the sides of the sink, Kai notices something strange about her eyes.

"What the hell?" she exclaims aloud.

Quickly covering her mouth and checking if anyone else is in the bathroom, Kai takes a few deep breaths and closes her eyes. When she opens them again, one of her eyes is now emerald green while the other is a deep blue with glowing orange and yellow rings around the pupils.

Why is this happening now? She wonders, feeling disgusted and frustrated as she hangs her head low. Retrieving her sunglasses from her purse, she quickly puts them on to shield her eyes and fixes her hair, trying to ignore the fluttering feeling in her stomach.

She walks back towards the counter, her gaze locks onto the man of her dreams. He is so handsome that all she wants to do is wrap her arms around him and kiss him with all her heart. He notices her and turns to watch as she approaches.

A smile spreads across his face, accentuating his dark mustache and goatee. She can't take her eyes off him, imagining herself sitting next to him and even jumping into his lap. Suddenly, he spins around and speaks to her.

"You're not from around here, are you?" he says. Kai tries to ignore him, but she is trembling with excitement inside.

He gently taps her on the shoulder, causing Kai to jump and turn around. She realizes it's him again, the man who can't seem to keep his hands or eyes off her. Nell interrupts their interaction by announcing that her food is ready, giving Kai a momentary sense of relief.

Kai gets up and walks over to the cash register, she feels another tap on her shoulder and turns to see him standing behind her. He compliments her on her gorgeous eyes before Nell interrupts again with her order. Kai tries to focus on completing her transaction, but he continues to engage with her. Finally, he asks for her name and she nervously replies "Kai".

Looking up through the top of her sunglasses at him, she can't help but feel flustered by his perfect grin and desirable scent. This stranger has a way of making her feel good and wanting more from him.

"Hello Kai, have you missed me?"

"What? Did you just say that you missed me?" No, he couldn't possibly have said that. I must be going insane.' Kai thinks to herself.

"Heaven's no! I am Victor, and it's wonderful to meet you, Kai."

He takes her hand and kisses it, leaving Kai in a daze. She wishes that kiss was on her lips instead of her hand.

"Well, the pleasure is all mine, Victor."

Kai quickly grabs her bag and turns to leave when Victor says: "Perhaps our paths will cross again. It was a pleasure to meet you, Kai."

She turns and gives him a small smile before hurrying out of the door.

Kai hurries and gets into her car, she can't believe she didn't talk to him longer. She curses herself for not giving him her phone number, especially since she was so tempted to bring him back to the motel and make love to him. That's why she came here in the first place - that irresistible feeling he gives her. The burning flame inside of her won't stop, but deep down she knows it's not love, just lust. He still makes her heart race at the thought of him.

Victor watches as Kai drives out of the parking lot and then heads to his own car. He can't help but think that it's finally her - she has come for him. He knows he needs to find her and see if she will let him be with her.

Pulling into a parking spot in front of the motel, Kai grabs her food and walks inside. She closes the door and throws the sandwich on the table next to the TV before sitting down on the bed. She feels defeated, knowing that she missed out on someone she sees as the perfect guy for her. She can't even bring herself to eat her food because she is so disgusted with herself. Instead, she decides to go through her notes and make a list of things she wants to do during her stay.

Suddenly, there's a knock at the door. Kai rolls her eyes, thinking that this maid won't give up. She swings open the door and starts to say "I don't want any room service..."

Caught off guard, it wasn't the maid at the door. Instead, it was Victor standing there, gazing into her eyes.

"I can't believe you're here," she says abruptly, almost sounding angry.

"Oh, I'm sorry. If you don't want to speak with me, I'll leave," Victor responds, turning to walk away. Kai watches him go and can't believe he's actually here.

"No, wait," she calls out, running across the parking lot to grab his arm. "Please, I'm sorry. I thought you were the maid again. I don't want you to leave. Please stay."

Kai slides her hand down his arm and he takes it in his own, pulling her closer to him. She trembles from nerves at being so close to him.

"Are you sure you want me to stay?" Victor asks.

"Yes, I do. I've missed you," Kai replies, waiting anxiously for his response.

He smiles at her and says, "I knew you'd come to me. I've been trying to call you for a while now."

"I know. I could hear you and feel you, and your scent..." Kai interrupts him with a kiss. Victor leans down and kisses her back before sweeping her up in his arms and carrying her into her motel room.

# 19

## "APRIL SAXON"

ON A TUESDAY MORNING, John receives a call from his research assistant Ellie, asking for a meeting to discuss the latest information gathered from interviews conducted in the past week. Most of the interviews are longtime residents of Beaver Creek. She suggests meeting at Nell's Diner at 10:30 a.m.

John arrives at Nell's and sees Ellie approaching from her car parked next to his truck. They enter the diner and sit by the front windows. Ellie hands John two folders, each of them, containing her findings. John is impressed with how professionally she has organized the information, complete with bullet points and descriptions of each person interviewed

John also asks Ellie about her hours so he can compensate her for her time last week. She hands him a detailed breakdown of her schedule, including the exact times she left her house, commuted to different locations, and conducted research or interviews.

"Your presentation is very well put together, Ellie. You have a talent for organizing information," John remarks.

"Thank you, I learned that in my first year of college. We had to learn how to prepare research for attorneys," Ellie responds.

She turns to the first page and begins explaining her interview with April May Brooks, one of the Saxons. "April is the youngest daughter of Martha Saxon, who inherited the property from her grandmother Clara." Ellie goes on to detail her conversation with April.

"She told me about her grandfather, who went missing while hunting on the property. Despite a week-long search, he was never found. The only thing that was discovered was his rifle, leaning against the old walnut tree where George Stellar was hanged. April believes this happened in the 1940s, but she wasn't completely sure."

Ellie fills John in on the family's unspoken secrets. According to April, when she was 17 years old, she and some friends went into their field at night during a full moon to catch fireflies. As they were counting their catches, they heard a high-pitched scream that didn't sound like any animal they knew. Curiosity getting the best of them, they ventured further into the woods towards Devil's Attic, where April's brother had previously fallen in. Through the bushes, they saw what appeared to be a squatting man with grey skin and a black stripe down its back. They soon noticed a woman approaching it, who seemed to have a perfect body but glowing pink eyes. Both the creature and the woman were unaware of their presence.

"That's when they realized it wasn't human and was carrying something. When it reached the grey creature, it pulled out a small body and placed it in front of itself. That's when things got unreal. They saw that the body was that of a young girl; her long blonde hair hung down as if she were asleep."

"Upon further inspection, they also noticed that the female figure was not human. Its hands were long and thin, with sharp claws measuring 2-3 inches. As they watched from the side, they saw its jaw unhinge like a snake, revealing rows of teeth ready to tear into its prey. And tear into the body it did, devouring it like a cougar feasting on its kill."

Ellie admits to John that she had doubts while listening to this story, but she reminds herself to keep an open mind. The more details April shared, the more convincing she became.

"She explained that after witnessing this gruesome scene, they all panicked and ran across the field as fast as possible, dropping their fireflies and nets in the process. In the midst of their escape, they heard screeching and howling noises, along with high-pitched screams. April compared the howling to coyotes rounding up their pack for a hunt. The sound of breaking twigs and rumbling feet filled their ears. April screamed for her parents as they ran through the field and into their house, locking the doors behind them. Huddled in her room, they armed themselves with whatever was available and waited for the creatures to break in."

John commented on how frightening this must have been for the children, and Ellie agreed, sharing how they took turns peeking out of the window to check for the creatures all night.

"The next week, a news article reported on a missing girl who disappeared while camping nearby."

Ellie mentioned that April and her friends said they'd never mention it ever again.

John asked why they didn't report it, realizing that it could have been the same girl who went missing during their encounter with the creatures.

"I asked that question too," Ellie says.

"April had told me that they were too scared to speak up. They believed that no one would believe their story, and they would be locked away in a mental institution for being crazy. In the Southern states, strange events like this are not taken lightly. Instead of being acknowledged by big cities like in the North, they would most likely be accused of being involved or even killing the girl themselves. April was probably right; it was best to keep quiet and keep it within the family as a dark secret."

"Ellie explained to John that April was worried about the story getting out after all these years, and had requested confidentiality from Ellie. She didn't want any trouble. I assured her that I wouldn't reveal anything she shared," Ellie added.

"It's a fascinating yet terrifying story," John replied to Ellie.

"You did great work."

"Thank you. It is very interesting to learn the truth about these urban legends that been around here for so many years."

He handed her four hundred dollars and some extra cash for gas since she had been driving around a lot for this case. Ellie informed John that she was going to interview an elderly woman in her eighties at the Golden Years Nursing Home on Highway 90 at 2:00 pm today. This woman was rumored to know stories about the Stellar family.

John and Ellie stand up from the table at the diner, preparing to leave. As they head towards the register, John scans the room and notices someone staring at him with a smile on their face.

"How are you, Mr. Smith?" the person calls out from across the room.

"Oh hey, Victor! I'm doing well, how about you?" John responds.

"I'm good, thanks for asking. By the way, we should catch up over dinner sometime," Victor suggests.

"Sure, sounds good. I'll give you a call." John agrees.

As they walk out of the diner and towards the parking lot, Ellie asks John who that person was. John tells her about his history with Victor and how they first met. Ellie warns John to be careful around Victor as some people believe he has dark powers and isn't as nice as he seems. John laughs it off, but Ellie's worried expression makes him realize she is serious.

"Don't worry, I'll watch my back around him," John reassures her.

Ellie nods and gets into her car to go to her appointment.

As Ellie pulls out of the parking lot, she glances at the diner's entrance and sees Victor standing there, watching her go. His smile seems to hold a secret, and he even waves at her. But Ellie quickly turns away, not wanting to make eye contact with him. She can't stand Victor; she used to have a crush on him, but after one lunch date, she became scared of him. Ever since then, she has been avoiding him.

# 20

## "WYNONA"

ELLIE DRIVES into the Golden Years Nursing Home, just a few miles away from Nell's diner. The building is made of yellow bricks and has a convenient drive-through entrance with a tall, rounded roof to protect visitors from the weather. She walks through a short pathway surrounded by flowers and live potted trees, leading up to the front doors and a lobby with an aquarium full of colorful fish.

The lobby itself is painted in relaxing mural of fields of flowers painted on one wall and pastel blue, accented with white trim, and scented with floral deodorizers. The overall ambiance is refreshing and inviting.

Ellie approaches the front desk, Ellie is greeted by the clerk who asks her to sign in and specify who she is there to visit. Ellie mentions Wynona, but doesn't know her last name. The clerk then informs her that it is Wynona Emanuel, a woman of American Indian and Spanish American descent who was born and raised in Beaver Creek since 1925.

A while later, a heavy-set man emerges from a side door connecting the lobby to the nursing home corridors. He calls out for Ellie and she follows him back through the corridor to meet Wynona. Wynona is sitting in a wheelchair dressed up as if going to church on a Sunday morning, with perfectly curled hair and pressed peach pants matched with a cream-colored blouse adorned with delicate white ruffles around the collar.

"Hello Wynona, I'm Ellie," says Ellie as she walks alongside the orderly pushing the wheelchair towards the garden.

The garden is filled with an array of blooming flowers of different colors, neatly groomed bushes, and well-maintained grass.

"The landscaping here is beautiful," comments Ellie before asking Wynona if she would mind discussing the Saxon property with her.

Wynona responds that she has no issue talking about it. Ellie then asks if she knows anything about the Stellar family, to which Wynona replies that she knows some stories about them.

Eager to get started, Ellie sets her iPad down and turns on the voice recorder so she can document their conversation.

Wynona reveals that the property is cursed, and anyone who resides there is unwelcome by the Native American spirits who inhabit the nearby creek.

"I was warned about this as a young girl," Wynona shares with a somber tone.

"There are other creatures living in the woods and caves besides the Native American spirits. Shapeshifters and beasts that prey on humans. The spirits drive away any people who try to live on the land. That's why Anne Stellar had to seek help from a gypsy woman in town. She and her family built their house too close to the creek, angering the sacred spirits and desecrating an Indian burial ground."

"Anne was accused of witchcraft and burned at the stake in town. Her husband George was also found guilty of harboring a witch and was hanged from the old walnut tree."

Ellie inquired about the two Stellar children. Wynona informs her that one girl was killed while the other ran away. The Marshal's men searched for her but couldn't find her, causing great distress for their leader. According to Wynona, anyone who dies on that property will haunt it forever.

"Marshal Crane was my great uncle, but he wasn't well-liked in our family due to his ruthless nature. He never married or had children, and his men were just like him. The townspeople had a history of finding missing persons on the property down the road. The victims were always mangled, as if they had been attacked by a wild animal. A hunting party was organized to track down the creature responsible, but nothing was ever found. Rumors circulated of eerie howls and shrill screams coming from the woods, scaring people away from traveling through at night. Eventually, a woman and her teenage son arrived on the stagecoach from Massachusetts to take up residence in the abandoned Stellar family home. The young man captured the attention of every girl in town with his striking looks, long dark hair, hazel eyes with yellow rings around them that seemed to see right into one's soul. He spoke perfect English without any trace of an accent, while his mother wore black and kept her face hidden behind a veil. The women of the town couldn't help but admire him whenever he came into town to run errands for himself and his mother. His perfectly muscled chest and flat stomach were always on display as he strolled through town with unbuttoned shirts tucked into his pants. Despite his European roots and charming demeanor, he fit in perfectly with the small-town community and left quite an impression on all who saw him."

"The town folk began filling uneasy about them no matter how handsome the young man was. They quickly became outcasts. The son would often go into town with his mother to trade herbs for supplies at the General Store. However, because she rarely spoke to anyone and always wore black, the townsfolk began to view them as witches. One night, my great uncle who was the town's Marshal went missing on his way home. He was never found, but his horse was discovered tied to the same walnut tree where George Stellar had been hanged years ago. A new Marshal took over after my great uncle's disappearance. They posted a wanted poster for the son of the outcast family throughout the town. The Marshal and his men found him working on a neighboring farm and arrested him for practicing black magic. They then sentenced him to be burned at the stake on the very farm he was working on. His mother arrived too late to save him and only requested to take his body back home for burial. The burnt body was loaded onto a wagon by the Marshal and returned to their property per the mother's request. From that day on, the town labeled them as cursed and avoided them at all costs."

Ellie inquires about the whereabouts of the mother.

"No one had seen the mother in a long time, maybe a year or more. But then one day she appeared at the General Store, trying to barter or sell her homemade herbal teas. The store owner accepted them and traded for some goods before sending her on her way. Later, he reported the incident to the Marshal who immediately rode out to the woman's house. He broke down the door and dragged her out by her hair. Witnesses claimed she was speaking in a strange language as if cursing everyone and the land. They deemed her a witch and began to tie her hands to a stake. But something unexpected happened - she began to change. Her face and eyes transformed color, and she grew unnaturally strong. It took several men to contain her, but they eventually got her on her knees and beheaded her."

"They didn't burn her?" Ellie asks.

No, they didn't have the chance. They dismembered her body and scattered the parts so she could never return."

"That's quite a story, Wynona," Ellie remarks.

"Excuse me for a moment, please? I need to use the restroom." Wynona signals for an orderly to assist her.

The orderly guides Wynona to the nurse's station inside the building before taking her to the bathroom. Ellie enters and asks the orderly for directions to the water fountain. He accompanies her, and along the way he casually mentions that Wynona tends to exaggerate stories.

"We have had some issues with her family because of it, which is why she ended up in the nursing home."

This news shocks Ellie, who was hoping for reliable information from Wynona. After using the bathroom, Wynona joins them with the nurse and asks if Ellie needed anything else.

"It's actually one more question, if you don't mind," says Ellie.

Wynona agrees and they sit outside in the sunny garden area. The fragrant scents of roses and jasmine fill the air, with hummingbird feeders scattered around. Taking in the beauty of her surroundings under the bright sun, Ellie remarks.

"I didn't realize how stunning this place was until now. The sunlight really brings out the colors of all these plants and flowers."

"Yes this is one reason why I love this place."

Ellie inquires Wynona about the missing Stellar girl. "Do you have any information on her whereabouts?"

Wynona relays what she has learned from various individuals over the years about Mary Stellar, the girl who disappeared without a trace. She explains that there is an urban legend surrounding Mary, which has been around since she was a child.

"In the 1850s, some hunters heard screams near Beaver Creek and went to investigate, thinking someone was being harmed. They crept quietly and found something unimaginable- the girl who was wanted by posters all over town, but now she appeared to be older- around 17 or 18 years old."

"Peeking from behind fallen trees, they saw a 'creature' attacking her. It was a grey, hairless being with red eyes and webbed arms resembling bat wings. They noticed it had bitten her neck and was still biting her as they approached. They were stunned by what they witnessed. The girl appeared unconscious and defenseless against the creature's attack.

After coming to their senses, the men noticed that the creature had caught wind of their presence and was now looking back at them. They quickly realized they needed to take action and shoot it down. Hurriedly, they grabbed their guns, but before they could aim, the creature made a sudden move and captured Mary in its grasp. It flew away with her high above the trees and out of sight. Despite their efforts to chase after them, they soon lost track of the creature."

"Did they ever find Mary?" asks Ellie.

"No," replies Wynona.

"That was the only time she was ever seen. They left up missing posters for a few months, but eventually the Marshal decided to take them down. The hunters' accounts led him to believe she was most likely dead. They searched extensively for both Mary and the creature, but neither were found. Some believe the hunter's made up the story to get notoriety, some say they just plane lied about it. And some say they were up there drinking to much mountain whiskey."

"Thank you so much for sharing this information with me and for meeting with me today," says Ellie gratefully.

"Oh, it's my pleasure dear. You're welcome to visit anytime and ask any more questions you may have. I enjoy the company," replies Wynona kindly. As they part ways, Ellie gives Wynona a hug goodbye.

# 21

## "I'M NOT DREAMING"

IN ROOM 12 of the Monticello Motel, Victor carries Kai and gently lays her on the bed. For the first time, she can fully admire the man she has dreamt about for so long. His hazel green eyes are framed by his black hair that falls just above his shoulders. He has a neatly groomed goatee and sideburns tracing his jawline. Slowly, he unbuttons his shirt and tosses it onto a nearby chair before removing his pants and climbing onto the bed with her.

His chest is perfectly muscular and covered in soft hair that Kai can't resist touching. His hand travels up her stomach to her breasts, she can feel her desire building inside her. When he bites her nipple, she can no longer hold back she yells Victor I want you so bad."

Feeling like she must be dreaming, Kai harshly pinches her outer thigh to check. But no, this is real. "What's wrong?" Victor asks.

"Nothing, I just thought I might be dreaming again," Kai replies.

"You don't find me attractive?"

"Oh my, you're..."

He leans closer to her and passionately kisses her, as if he had been waiting for this moment for a long time. She eagerly returns the kiss with equal fervor. Embracing each other she can't help but think back to all the dreams she's had of kissing him. It is a powerful and romantic feeling to finally have his lips against hers.

She reaches up and pulls him towards her, wanting to be as close to him as possible. He runs his hand up her thigh and between her legs, eliciting a gasp and a moan from her. She breaks away from his mouth and trails kisses down his neck, making soft sounds of approval. With his fingers inside her, she quivers and moans in pleasure.

"Oh Victor, you're going to make me..." She climaxes.

He removes his hand and moves down to pleasure her with his tongue, but she stops him and pulls him closer.

"I need you; I want you," she tells him urgently. "I want to feel you inside me now."

He reaches up and grabs her breast, suckling on one while she throws her head back in pleasure. Her desire for him is driving her wild, causing her to breathe fast and short. Each touch of his hand on her body sends her into a frenzy; the sensation of him rubbing her nipple and biting the other makes her feel lightheaded. She's never felt this kind of passion with anyone before, and it's intense enough to make her want to dig her nails into his skin and sink her teeth into him. She can't explain where these urges are coming from. He continues to caress and kiss her, she can't resist any longer and grabs his shaft and puts it inside her. He helps by thrusting himself in her.

"Yes, harder, Victor," she begs. "I want you all the way inside me."

He thrusts harder into her as she voices her pleasure for it. He spins her around and up on top of him sliding his shaft again inside her as she pushes down on it.

He runs his hands down her hips and lifts her up as she leans forward to kiss him. Unable to hold back any longer, she bites his neck as he thrusts harder into her. She moans in pleasure as she moves in sync with him. He holds onto her hips as he rolls her over onto her back, never breaking their connection.

With each movement, they both become more consumed by their desire.

"Take me," she whispers in his ear. "Devour me, please. I can't hold back any longer."

He obeys, pushing himself harder and deeper each time he moves inside of her. She gasps as he brings her too climax again and again, screaming in pure ecstasy with each powerful thrust.

Letting out a joyful scream, he gazes down at her in awe. As she opens her eyes and looks back up at him, he notices a change in their color - one is now a deep emerald green with a fiery orange ring around the pupil, while the other is a deep blue with the same fiery hues. He can feel the heat radiating from her body as he enters her deeply. She lets out another high-pitched cry of pleasure as she reaches climax once again. He feels her hot breath on his skin and her nails digging into his back, urging him to go faster. As he thrusts harder, he too reaches his peak and spills his seed inside her.

Still lost in each other's embrace, he slowly pulls out and moves to lie beside her. Placing his hand on her stomach, he can feel how warm and sweaty she is. As he lifts his head to ask her something, he notices that her hair is gradually lightening from black to almost blonde. Propping himself up on one arm, he watches in amazement as a shimmer of silver light dances over her body, causing it to undergo strange changes.

Her muscles bulge and grow in her limbs, and her nails transform into sharp claws like those of a small canine. Even her feet elongate and sprout white fur.

He watches as she trembles uncontrollably before suddenly returning to her human form in one swift movement. Gazing into her face, he asks if she knows what is happening.

"I feel faint," she gasps, "but this intense desire burns inside me whenever you're near me. What is going on?"

He notices a change in her, as if she is trying to become something else. He can't quite put his finger on it, but he knows she is a shifter. She shakes her body and a shimmer of light flashes, revealing her transformation: part human, part fox. It's her first time shifting, and she is struggling to control it. He looks at her face and sees that her mouth has shifted into a dog-like muzzle with sharp canine fangs. Her jawline has extended, making room for the changes. As she continues to shift, her hair turns pure white and falls just below her breasts, leaving her nipples exposed. She moans and writhes in discomfort as the transformation progresses.

"You're incredible," he tells her in amazement. "The most beautiful creature I've ever laid eyes on."

Kai's temperature rises and she shakes again, this time transforming back into human form much more smoothly. He encourages her to keep practicing until it becomes second nature.

She groans and moves her legs in pain, feeling the strain of the transformation.

"Victor, I need you," she whispers in his ear, her lips brushing against his skin. He can feel her desire, her need for him. She straddles him, kissing him all the way down his body until she takes him into her mouth. He hesitates, afraid of being bitten, but she soothes his fears with her hand and tongue. Soon, he becomes fully erect again and she climbs on top of him, taking control as she forces him inside of her. In a frenzy of passion, they change positions, and he enters her from behind, making her scream in pleasure. They climax together before collapsing onto the bed in exhaustion.

He gently wipes away the sweat from her face with a cool cloth as she rests in his arms. But suddenly, she sits up and paces around the room. In one glance she suddenly shifts into a pure white fox and paces in a circle. Victor quickly locks the door to prevent anyone from seeing her.

"Kai, are you okay?" he asks with concern.

She doesn't respond, just stares straight ahead pacing. She stops for a moment staring at the door before turning and facing Victor. She starts to transform back to human.

Eventually, she settles down and they both fall back onto the bed.

He takes her hand and gently pulls her towards him. He gently caresses her stomach and hand. Suddenly, she starts to shake and the glimmering light around her intensifies before she passes out. Victor grabs her so she doesn't hit the floor. Her body starts to jerk as if she is having a seizure.

"Kai, Kai!" Victor calls out to her.

"Are you okay? Can you hear me?" He lifts her up and lays her down in the center of the bed. Grabbing some wet, cool towels, he places them on her forehead. Climbing into bed next to her, he holds her close. Slowly, she opens her eyes and looks at him with a faint smile.

"There you are, you had me worried," Victor says with relief.

"What happened?"

"You shifted. Didn't you feel it coming?"

"No, it's all a blur. I remember feeling hot, but it seemed like a nightmare."

"You shifted multiple times and each time, you were the most stunning creature I've ever seen."

"What did I shift into?"

"I'm not entirely sure, but you appeared to be like a fox woman that is part human and part fox. Your hair was pure white, and your eyes were different colors. You were breathtaking."

A Kitsune is a type of Japanese shifter that transforms into a white fox, also known as White Bone Spirit - a captivating sprite.

Kai is unaware of her family history from her father's side. Although he is Chinese and Japanese, he never spoke much about his past or childhood to Kai.

"He embraced my mother's American Indian beliefs and became so enamored with the heritage that he forgot about his troubled past and fully immersed himself in the tribe." Kai shares with Victor, discussing her father.

With a fusion of both her parents' DNA and cultural backgrounds, she may possess unique shape-shifting abilities.

As Kai drifts off to sleep, Victor quietly gets up, gets dressed, and leaves Room 12. He gently closes the door behind him, then hangs a "Do Not Disturb" sign on the outside so that the maid won't disturb her. He walks to his car, he hears someone call out his name.

"Victor, what are you doing at a motel?" Mrs. Jones asks.

"Oh, hello Mrs. Jones. It's lovely to see you again."

"You have a lady friend locked up in that room, don't you Victor Donovan?"

"Well, you caught me. She's a friend from Virginia who came to visit me. How have you been, Mrs. Jones?"

"I've been well."

"What brings you here?"

"The owners want to sell this place, so they hired me to list it for them. I'm just taking some photos."

"Well, have a good day."

"You take care now, Victor."

Victor drives away from the parking lot and heads back to his office.

Out of all the people who could have seen me leaving a motel, it had to be Debra Jones - known as the 'mouth of the South' for her gossiping ways. Damn.

# 22

## "SPIRITS IN THE MIST"

JOHN AND HURLEY make a trip into town to collect some packages from the post office, including additional night vision wildlife cameras that they plan to place inside the cave. With the help of Sheriff Taylor, they hope to catch a glimpse of whatever is lurking inside and potentially uncover the identity of the murderer responsible for the recent deaths.

At the post office, John hands over his tickets to the clerk who brings out three large boxes and one small box.

"This one requires your signature, Mr. Smith."

After signing for the package, John carries them out to his truck and places them in the back seat. He then takes the small box and brings it into the front with him. Inside the truck, he uses his knife to carefully open the box. Inside, there is a white deerskin with a symbol etched onto the front. The piece is about two inches wide and four inches long, held together by a strap cinched at the top to prevent any contents from falling out. John picks it up and examines it closely. It appears to have Native American origins, but he can't figure out why someone would send this to him. As he looks closer, he notices a small note rolled up tightly and tied with sweet grass. He grabs it and unties the knot before unrolling the note.

*I have heard of your land and the restless spirits that reside within it. Our ancestors have protected that area for many moons, allowing both good and evil to coexist in this sacred place. This creates a portal to other realms, making it a dangerous place for unprotected humans to enter. As a medicine man, I have created something for you to always carry with you as protection from the malevolent beings that dwell in your caves and on the land. It has been blessed and contains powerful herbs with supernatural properties that will ward off any harmful spirits.*
*Dr. Jacy Redbone,*
*Medicine* Man

John grins at Hurley and says, "Looks like we have someone watching over us, boy."

He starts his truck and drives out of the parking lot, calling the sheriff's office on the way to inform them that he has retrieved the cameras and is heading back to the camper.

Pulling up to the garage, John sees that all of the CSI investigators have left the back pasture. They must have collected the body and any evidence they needed. He ponders whether or not the sheriff was right about the identity of the body, and if it really is the boy who went by the creek.

John heard a voice inside his head urging him to set up cameras inside the cave to uncover the source of the strange occurrences. So, he opens the door and calls for Hurley to come with him.

His phone rings, and it's the sheriff returning his call. They agree to meet tomorrow morning to install the cameras, with Deputy Fred covering for the sheriff at the office.

John starts preparing the cameras by inserting SD cards and batteries and labeling them for easier organization. With one camera left to set up, he notices that it's already 6:45 p.m. Realizing how quickly the day has gone by, John decides to wrap up and have dinner with Hurley before watching some TV together.

Later on, after their meal and cleaning up, John takes a shower and reflects on how there have been no disturbances from shifters or spirits since he moved into the garage with his camper. Instead of watching TV as planned, he decides to review the videos from his outdoor surveillance cameras to see if there's any activity worth noting.

After stepping out of the shower and settling in front of his computer, he connects the USB cable from the recorder to his laptop. He hits the fast forward button, watching as days turn into nights and back again on the recording. The only thing captured is some wildlife moving through the field.

As days pass by, the sun sets, and a thick fog appears in the tree line. He knows what lies within that fog: shifters and spirits. Quickly jotting down the time on the recording, he watches as the fog rolls closer, resembling waves in an ocean. Suddenly, white ghostly streaks shoot out of the thick fog like a wave of water, darting around the field with boundless energy. They playfully circle and spin, seeming to put on a show for an audience. John watches how much they have changed since he put the fallen warrior to rest. He wonders if this is all thanks to achieving peace amongst them. Two animal spirits dance closer towards the garage's front camera, John laughs at their playful behavior before they disappear into thin air.

Suddenly, a figure appears in front of one camera while another one pops up on the other camera. These beings can shift between forms, taking on the appearance of spirit animals. Their upper half resembles a coyote while their lower half is human. They have striking amber eyes that seem to glow in the darkness. They float in front of the cameras with a sense of peace and non-aggression towards John. Then, just as quickly as they appeared, they disappear into the shadows. But more shifters emerge from behind them, forming a line like warriors preparing for battle. John leans closer to the screen, captivated by this strange phenomenon.

"They're creating a barrier, but for what?" he whispers.

He watches the lines of spirit animals multiply and cover every angle on the cameras, he reaches for the small package he received in the mail. Inside is a white deer skin bag with a single beaver claw tied to it. Whoever sent this must have a connection to these spirit animals. How else could all of this be happening? John realizes that these people are deeply spiritual and connected to the earth and it's creatures. He holds onto the bag tightly as he witnesses the shifters acting as if they are defending his garage against some unseen threat. But what could it be? What danger do they perceive that he cannot see? As a few shifters fly above the lines and over the field like scouts in battle, John can't help but wonder what they are protecting him from.

Unable to see past the lines of ghostly spirit animals, John waits and observes. He notices more of them take off in an almost charging stance towards something in the field. The others break formation and begin circling the garage. There must be hundreds of them by now. They keep flying out to the field and attacking something. John squints, trying to get a closer look.

"Holy shit! It's that black entity!" he exclaims out loud.

Every spirit animal that tries to attack it seems to have no effect. They don't even slow it down. It just keeps moving towards the garage, completely unfazed by their attacks. More and more spirit animals join in, hitting it harder and faster, but it continues to move towards the garage as if they aren't even there. Suddenly, the spirit animals form a shape in front of the garage, molding together and growing taller until John can finally make out what it is.

"It's a giant grizzly bear! It's huge!" John yells in excitement. The bear spirits begin moving towards the black entity, ready to challenge it. As they get closer, John notices a bright light flashing like a big camera flash. "What the hell is that?" he wonders aloud.

Mesmerized by what he's seeing on the recording, John watches as the bear spirit animal gets tossed to the side by the black entity, only to quickly get back up and stand in front of it again. The spirit bear raises its left arm and swings it towards the entity, another bright white flash shooting out across the field. Despite this attack, the bear spirit remains standing just outside of range from the garage lights and cameras. As John searches for any sign of the black entity, he suddenly notices two red glowing eyes forming on the right side of the bear spirit. It's still there after all of that.

The dark figure charges towards the bear spirit animal, but suddenly transforms into a different shape. It becomes a Native American warrior, adorned in a traditional a shield and headdress. The once ghostly white entity now has vibrant colors and takes on the form of a giant warrior, standing guard in front of the garage. I wonder if this is the same warrior I discovered and laid to rest, returning to protect me from the malevolent black entity.

The warrior stands tall as the black entity swiftly moves towards him. He raises his shield and a bright amber light shoots out, striking the black entity and sending it flying through the air. The warrior advances towards the struggling entity as it regains its footing and stares back at him. With a fierce charge, the black entity rushes towards the warrior, who waits until it's almost upon him before swinging his shield with great force. Thunder reverberates through the field as lightning cracks through the air, causing the black entity to be thrown even further than before.

After a moment lying on the ground, the black entity rises once again. The Native warrior points towards a nearby creek and the black entity turns to look before turning back to face the warrior. Without hesitation, it retreats towards the creek and away from the garage.

"Did you see that Hurley? They defeated the evil spirit!" John exclaims with excitement, jumping up from his seat.

The Native warrior turns and walks towards the garage, his gaze fixed on the cameras. John's eyes follow his every move. The warrior stands in front of the camera, a formidable figure with a direct look into the lens. "A'he'hee," he says, expressing gratitude to the camera.

John sinks back into his chair, realizing the significance of those words. They were thanking him for burying their fallen comrade. Oh my god, John thinks to himself.

Still facing the camera, the Native warrior steps back and raises his arms to his sides. A faint white smoke surrounds him before he suddenly breaks apart into all the spirit animals that had previously appeared on the field. They circle and race around as if they have achieved victory.

John smiles and speaks to the camera, "Well done, guys! Thank you!"

The fog recedes and they follow it out to the middle of the field before vanishing into the darkness of the tree line.

"That was incredible, Hurley. They are looking out for us. I can't believe it. This is like nothing I've ever experienced before. We should probably keep this between us for the protection of these Native American spirits and their animal counterparts."

John fast forwards through the rest of the recording, watching as day turns into night and then back again. He notices that when the fog is not present, wild animals roam freely around the pasture near the garage. But when the fog rolls in, they stay away from the field as if sensing something sacred there.

# 23

## "THE POND"

At 5:30 a.m., Hurley wakes John up with his whining to go outside. John groggily makes his way to the kitchen and pours himself a cup of coffee to start his day. Today, he and Sheriff Taylor will be installing cameras inside the cave on their property. As he waits for the coffee to cool down, John turns on the TV to check the weather forecast and settles into his recliner.

A loud bark at the door interrupts his peaceful morning routine. Hurley has returned from his outdoor excursion and is ready to come back inside. But when John opens the door, to see Hurley standing in the driveway, looking up at John expectantly.

"Come on, Hurley," John urges, but the dog just sits there and stares at him. "I'm not dressed yet for a mule ride around the property, boy."

But Hurley keeps barking and nudging something towards John. Realizing that Hurley must have found something important, John quickly puts his shoes on and walks out to the driveway where Hurley is.

Flicking on the flash light, John sees what Hurley has found - another bone! But this time, it looks like a human arm bone with a hand still attached. And upon closer inspection, John notices that one finger is missing - the ring finger.

Excitement and dread flood through John as he realizes what this could mean - could this be connected to the mysterious disappearance of someone on their property? Without a doubt, this could be crucial evidence in solving the case.

"Where did you find this, Hurley? Can you show me?"

John gestures for Hurley to follow him as he walks out towards the field. Hurley trots alongside John and looks out into the vast expanse of greenery.

"Show me where you found it, Hurley."

Hurley turns and looks towards the area where the cave is.

"Well let's go see boy." John gets in the mule and Hurley takes him across the field, down the path and to the old Stellar foundation.

"Did you find the bone here, boy?" Hurley barks and spins in a circle, confirming John's suspicion that this was indeed where he found it. But why do human bones keep turning up in this spot? What could it mean?

John heads back to the garage and examines the bone. He grabs a plastic container and wraps the bone carefully in a towel before placing it high on a shelf, hidden from view.

"I better go get a shower the sheriff is coming to help install camera's today."

Getting everything ready to head out to install cameras in a nearby cave, Sheriff Taylor pulls up outside.

"Hop in, Sheriff," John says, motioning towards the passenger seat.

They drive off down the narrow logging road, heading towards Beaver Creek.

"It's quite a beautiful morning today," John comments as they make their way.

"Yes, it's been a nice stretch of dry weather with highs in the 70s," Sheriff Taylor agrees.

Hurley bounds alongside them through the tall grass, racing towards the creek. John turns at an old walnut tree and carefully makes his way down the path on his mule. Hurley is already splashing around in the shallow waters of the creek.

"I widened this path with my tractor and box blade so I could finally take the mule all the way down here. It was getting tiring carrying everything back and forth up the hill," John explains.

After parking the mule by the creek, they must wade through the water to reach the cave entrance. Luckily, the creek is low today or they would be wading waist deep.

Setting up and starting the generator, they unroll all of the electric cords needed to reach inside the large room of the cave. John carries in halogen lights while Sheriff Taylor brings a box of cameras. The sheriff motions with his flashlight for John to follow him. The Sheriff hands John a flashlight and gives him instructions.

"When I flash the light at you, hit the switch to turn on the lights. I want to see if anything moves in this room when the lights come on."

John quickly gets the lights plugged in and places his hand on the switch, ready for the signal from the Sheriff. As soon as the light flashes, John hits the switch and the room is flooded with light. They quickly scan the area for any movement as instructed by the Sheriff.

"Did you see that?" The Sheriff exclaims.

"See what?" John responds.

The Sheriff steps back and looks up, noticing a cliff and an opening above a granite table. He realizes that this is where the creature must have gone when it climbed up the wall. They both look up and see two red eyes peering down at them.

"Do you see those red eyes, Sheriff?"

"Yes, I do. That's our cave creature, watching us," replies the Sheriff.

He calls out to the creature, "Hey, Benny Saxon, is that you up there?" The red eyes disappear into the darkness.

"We'll have to be careful, John," warns the Sheriff. "We're trespassing in their territory and they won't take kindly to our noise and bright lights."

"I agree, Sheriff. We'll need to keep a lookout while we work."

Heading back to their mule, the Sheriff asks John if he saw the creature leap into the pond earlier.

"No, I didn't see it," replies John.

"I saw something in the water, it looked like a mermaid or a large fish," John explains to Sheriff Taylor.

"It had a teal blue and green tail and was partially submerged in the water. Could you imagine if there really was a mermaid living in this cave?"

"You certainly wouldn't want that getting out to the media," the sheriff responds.

"They would be swarming this place trying to capture it and sell it for profit."

John nods in agreement. "I've been finding a lot of things around here that should stay within these walls. Out of respect for the Native American spirits, their ancestors, and the creatures that inhabit this area, as well as the Stellar and Saxon families, I believe it's best to keep some things a secret."

The sheriff chuckles and pats John on the back.

"I couldn't agree more. Some things are better left untold for the protection of those involved. But let's keep that between us."

"Of course," John replies with a smile. "You're a good man, Sheriff Taylor." They share a laugh before continuing their search through the cave.

"We're two peas in a pod, John," they both laugh as they exit the cave to gather more supplies.

"Hurley, where are you boy?" John calls out as they reach the bottom of the hill. Hurley comes bouncing towards them, tail wagging happily.

Carrying the remaining supplies and ladders into the cave, John explains to the sheriff how he has labeled everything for easier tracking of camera locations.

After a few hours of work, they finally get to the last camera. While drilling holes to mount the bracket that will hold the camera in place, John adjusts its position while the sheriff surveys the area it needs to cover. Suddenly, the sheriff notices something dark in the water of the large pond. It's situated near where the granite table is and next to the tall wall leading to another opening in the cave.

"What do you think about this spot for the camera, Sheriff?"

"JOHN!"

"Yeah, what's going on?" John climbs off the ladder and walks over to where Sheriff Taylor is standing.

"There's something in the water." The sheriff points to a dark shape under the surface.

"Do you remember when we saw footprints entering and exiting the water before?" Sheriff Taylor asks John. John nods in confirmation.

"Well, there's something down there now and I saw a few air bubbles come up. Something's lurking under there." The sheriff speaks in a hushed tone. John takes a step towards the water, but Sheriff Taylor grabs his arm and stops him. He suggests letting the cameras capture whatever is hiding below instead.

"We have to pretend like we don't know it's in there, that way it will come out and the cameras will capture its movements through the cave," John whispered to Sheriff Taylor.

"Yeah, you're right. The element of surprise is key," confirmed the sheriff.

Without looking back, they both walked back towards the light. John grabbed all the necessary tools and equipment while Sheriff Taylor carried the lights and cords behind him. They loaded everything onto a mule and headed back to the garage. Meanwhile, Hurley had already returned to the camper and was waiting at the door.

"Well, Sheriff, I'll check those cameras in a few days to make sure everything went smoothly. I'll switch out the SD cards as well and let you know if I find anything," said John.

"Thanks again for your help, John. Take care."

John pulled into the garage with the mule and told Hurley he would unload everything in the morning. He wanted to take a shower and relax before calling it a night. However, just as he was about to enter his house, his cell phone rang.

"Hurley...it's Momma," John said, glancing at his phone. His wife Lizzie usually called later in the night unless something was wrong.

# 24

## "THE FIND"

ELLIE PULLS UP in front of the Beaver Creek library, ready to continue her research into the Stellars and the mysterious events surrounding them. She's starting to believe that there is truth behind all the strange occurrences at John's place. After speaking with many people and finding more information, she can't dismiss it any longer. The existence of different creatures and beings has been recorded in history for thousands of years, including urban legends like Mary Stellar and Benny Saxon. She hasn't told John about these legends because she always thought they were just stories. But after reading some proven books, she's willing to open her mind to the possibility that these events are real. She believes that whatever is on John's property has been there for a long time but is only now being brought into the light as technology has changed the society becoming more accepting of these beings.

They are the dark shadows we sometimes catch in our peripheral vision, the figures we see standing in the trees, and the unsettling presence that makes us feel watched while wandering through the woods of Beaver Creek.

After hours of sifting through old newspapers on microfiche, Ellie finally finds a picture of the missing Stellar girls from 1849. The article reveals that U.S Marshal Isaac Crane and his men had taken the girls into custody while they were on their way to the church orphanage. However, the girls managed to escape and ran into the nearby woods. According to rumors, they were then assaulted by the deputies. When the men caught them at the edge of Beaver Creek, things took a turn for the worse. Some of the deputies attempted to assault the girls as well, but one of them managed to break free and run across the creek. She watched in horror as her sister was being attacked before disappearing into the woods herself, never to be seen again. The men claimed that they never touched the youngest girl, but during their rescue attempt, a grayish creature with human-like features emerged from the water behind her. It had slimy skin and prominent bones, webbed hands with long claws, and coal-black eyes emitting a foul odor. Marshal Crane returned with the girls, and a closed room trial was conducted with law enforcement and government officials present to make a decision.

According to the three men's testimony, a strange creature emerged from the water and dragged Molly beneath its depths. The two other men rushed in to save her, but she was already unconscious by the time they brought her back to shore. After hearing all three testimonies, the court declared that the Deputy Marshals were not guilty of child abuse or Molly's disappearance. They concluded that unknown circumstances had occurred beyond their control. Ellie scoffs at the verdict and continues digging through old newspapers. She finds something interesting in an 1853 obituary mentioning a retired Deputy Marshal who was found dead while hunting alone. Three years later, another one of Marshal Crane's men met a similar fate while out hunting with his daughter. Their bodies were discovered torn apart and unrecognizable in a small cave on Sulfur Mountain. Despite the gruesome scene, their identities were confirmed through pieces of clothing found nearby.

While taking notes and scouring through old newspapers, Elle discovers yet another retired Deputy Marshal who was murdered eight years later. This time, it was a father and his two sons who were killed while out hunting for deer. Just like the previous case, they disappeared without a trace until one of the search party members stumbled upon a partially covered body in the brush. After an extensive search, they found the other two bodies, torn apart but not as badly as the first attack. The town sent out hunters to track down the animal responsible, but they never found anything.

Still determined, Ellie continues her research and comes across an obituary for one of the deputy's daughters. She vanished in 1873 while walking home from a friend's house and was found dead a few days later, ruled as a wild animal attack by wolves.

As she reads this, Ellie can't help but notice that every person involved in the killing of the Stellers had been brutally murdered themselves. It seems that only the families related to the Stellar incident were targeted. She writes down their names and dates, realizing that these killings began after George Stellar's execution, Mary's escape, and Molly's death. It dawns on her that Mary must have died alone in the woods all those years ago; she wouldn't have survived living on her own at such a young age.

Ellie's first question is always, "How did this all get overlooked?" She spends hours scouring the obituary section of newspapers each year, adding names to her growing list of missing or attacked descendants of Deputy Marshals. But it wasn't until she stumbled upon Abigail Flynn's recent disappearance and subsequent grisly death in Beaver Creek that things started to click into place for Ellie. Like the others before her, Abigail's body was believed to be torn apart by a wild animal.

With her pencil finally set down, Ellie knows she needs to contact John immediately. He was the one who had discovered

Abigail's remains on his property, after all. So she sends him a text, insisting they meet as soon as possible because she has crucial information to share.

As Ellie waits for John's response, she props her head up with her arm and reads through her notes, trying to organize everything coherently. "Who could be behind these killings?" she mumbles to herself, wondering if it could be a curse from Anne Stellar or perhaps the oldest daughter of one of the surviving deputies.

But still no word from John. Frustrated and eager to share her findings with someone else, Ellie packs up her things and heads home. She'll have to wait until tomorrow to speak with her boss about this new information.

She makes her way back, she starts brainstorming how she can trace any remaining descendants of the deputies. Maybe interviewing the Flynn family would provide more insight into their family history and other surviving relatives. Satisfied with her plan, Ellie eagerly awaits John's call so she can fill him in on everything she has uncovered.

Ellie smiles to herself, feeling a flutter of excitement in her stomach. This discovery would impress her boss and maybe even earn her a kiss. She couldn't help the small crush she had developed on him. As she drives home, she thinks about getting ready for their possible meeting later that night.

She parks her car and makes her way inside, already planning on what to wear to seduce him if he calls.

In her bedroom, she sets her book bag down on the bed before browsing through her wardrobe for something more alluring.

# 25

## "THE VISION"

Kᴀɪ ᴀᴡᴀᴋᴇɴs to the glow of her phone on the nightstand, its screen displaying 4:30 in the afternoon. She attempts to rise from bed and head to the bathroom, but a searing pain shoots through her head with each movement. Clutching her skull in agony, she can feel the pressure building from within as if someone is attempting to escape by pounding their way out. The sharp pains radiate from the back of her neck and head all the way to her eyes.

"Another migraine," she mutters as she winces and rubs her temples. She slowly inches towards the edge of the bed, careful not to exacerbate the pain. If only she could drill a hole into her skull and release the pressure.

Instead, she makes her way to the table where she keeps her migraine medicine in her purse. Struggling to open the bottle, she takes one pill and chases it down with a few sips of water from her bottle.

Lying back in bed, she turns on the TV for some distraction, but even the dim light causes excruciating pain behind her closed eyelids. She settles on the news channel, listening while clicking through channels until she finds something local.

After fifteen minutes, she realizes she needs to use the bathroom. She carefully swings her feet to the side of the bed and tries to stand up, but is immediately met with a sharp pain in her head. She hunches over, grabbing her head in agony. Slowly making her way to the bathroom, she grabs a wet washcloth on her way back to the bed. Placing the cool cloth on the back of her neck helps ease some of the pain and pressure.

As she waits for the migraine medication to kick in, Kai listens to the news. The local sheriff is giving a statement about a recent body found on Sulfur Mountain. It turns out to be the same young man who was reported missing by his friends. The cause of death is still unknown, but an update will be given once it's determined. The killer is still at large and anyone with information is urged to contact the sheriff's office.

Kai falls asleep thinking about the young man and how he died. Flashes of images play like a slideshow in her mind: A group of people walking together, a beautiful girl with long black hair, and then Kai standing in a field surrounded by crickets and other insects chirping under a bright full moon. Something moves in the grass and as she gets closer to investigate, she realizes it's the couple she saw earlier having sex. But then something changes - the girl's body transforms into a snake-like creature with long tail-like legs that wrap around the guy's legs. Kai watches this surreal scene unfold before her eyes.

She watches in horror as the girl leans down and sinks her teeth into the guy's neck. She sees him struggle and hears a gurgling sound as he chokes on his own blood. The girl's grip on his neck tightens, and Kai steps closer to get a better look. To her shock, she realizes that the girl is no longer human. Her eyes are glowing red, her jaw has elongated, and her fingers are now long and bony. With a long snake-like tongue, the creature feasts on the man's blood and fluids. Kai can hear bones cracking as the creature squeezes the man's skull between its hands. Feeling sick, Kai takes a step back as the creature transforms before her eyes.

The snake-like tails turn into human skin and move down the creature's body, leaving behind human legs in their wake. It's like watching dominos fall, except much faster and with a strange glowing effect. As the transformation completes, Kai notices that her hair has turned black once again after appearing white earlier. Stunned and confused, Kai mutters "What are you?" The creature pauses for a moment, almost as if it heard her question. And then, in a sudden flash of light, the body of the man shrivels up like a mummy while the creature's appearance changes back to that of a human.

As she watches, the woman stands up and pulls on her dress. She turns to leave, but pauses and looks back as if sensing someone watching her. However, she doesn't see anyone and soon disappears into the fog. The image fades away and Kai is once again focused on the TV screen in front of her.

"Thank goodness that's over," she sighs. As she gets dressed, Kai realizes she needs to inform the sheriff about the woman from her vision.

The migraine pill has finally relieved her head pain and Kai sits up on the edge of the bed. She knows she must speak to the sheriff about what she saw, but would he even believe her wild story? After taking a shower and getting dressed, Kai hears her phone ringing. It's Victor, but she decides to call him back later because she needs to get to the sheriff's office before they close.

Approaching the front desk at the office, Kai is greeted by a deputy who offers to help her. She explains that she needs to talk to the sheriff about the young man found on Sulfur Mountain. The deputy calls for the sheriff and tells Kai he will be out shortly. While waiting, Kai walks over to the nearby lobby and as she is about to sit down, Sheriff Taylor introduces himself.

"Hello Ms. Liu, I'm Sheriff Taylor. How can I assist you?" he asks.

"Hi Sheriff Taylor, my name is Kai Liu.

"I am a forensic technician for the DNA lab in Quantico, Virginia."

The sheriff interrupts and says, "That's where we send all evidence to be tested."

"Yes, that's correct."

"What brings you to Kentucky?" he asks.

"I was assigned to test some items that were sent to our lab from here. During the handling of these items, I became ill and two weeks later fell into a coma."

"I remember hearing about that. I'm glad to see you're doing better now."

"Thank you, Sheriff. Is there somewhere we can speak more privately?" Kai asks.

"Yes, ma'am, follow me to my office."

She follows him and takes a seat across from his desk.

"As I was saying, Sheriff Taylor, while handling your items, something strange happened. Please keep an open mind as I explain this to you."

Kai goes on to describe the events leading up to her arrival in Beaver Creek, leaving out any mention of Victor. She then explains the vision she just had at the motel and why she had to come talk to him. She saw the person responsible for the young man's death.

The sheriff leans forward in his chair and rubs his chin thoughtfully. "Ms. Liu, it's amazing that you're telling me this. I have interviewed the victim's friends and they gave the same description of the suspect that you just did. Do you know the victim?"

"No, sir, I never met him

"Have you had any contact with the victim's friends or family in the past couple of weeks?"

"No, sir. I don't know anyone in Kentucky. I just heard about the young man today on the local news station." Kai explains.

Kai reveals to him that she is part American Indian and has visions, this one being particularly disturbing as it felt very real. She sensed the energy and smell of sex from them.

"I witnessed the entire incident but was unable to move and help the young man. The creature the girl transformed into was unlike anything I've ever seen," she confesses.

"Since waking from my coma, the visions I have became stronger."

"I would like to visit the location where the body was found, Sheriff," Kai requests. She believes she may be able to track down the creature and make a connection with her mind to capture it before it strikes again.

Sheriff Taylor agrees to take her to the property after getting permission from the owner, John, who he believes will welcome her assistance given his knowledge of spirits and shifters in the woods.

"Here is my card, Sheriff. You can reach me on my cell phone and I'm staying at Room 12 in the Beaver Creek Motel for another eleven days," she informs him politely.

"I'll give you a call as soon as I hear from John," Sheriff Taylor says.

Kai reaches out and shakes Sheriff Taylor's hand before she walks out of the lobby.

Driving back to the motel, Victor calls her again. She answers, "Hello...yes, I'm on my way back to the motel. No, I haven't had dinner yet. I had some errands to run in town."

"I'm actually feeling great, better than I have in weeks. Sure, let's go out to dinner. What time do you want to pick me up? Seven works for me. See you then, bye."

She hangs up and pulls into the motel parking lot. In a hurry, she rushes into her room to change her shoes and grab a jacket. Just as she's walking out her door, she sees Victor pulling in and parking next to her car.

"Hey there, you look amazing!" he exclaims as he gets out of his car.

"Thank you, you look great too," Kai responds with a smile.

Victor walks into the room behind her, he chuckles and closes the door. She places the towels on the counter by the bathroom, then turns around to find Victor gently grabbing her and pressing his lips against hers in a warm hug.

"I missed you today," he whispers in her ear.

She responds with a passionate kiss, not knowing how else to express herself.

"Where are we going to eat?" she asks him. Victor replies that he's taking her to a fantastic Chinese restaurant that has been owned and run by the same family for years. He knows them well and wants her to meet some of them.

"I'm sure you'll love it," he assures her as they climb into his car and make their way to the Garden Chinese Restaurant down the road.

# 26

## "THE DATE"

AFTER FINISHING HIS SHOWER, John answers his phone to find Ellie requesting a meeting tonight in town to discuss important information. He suggests postponing until the next day, but Ellie insists on meeting over dinner. They agree to meet at the Chinese restaurant in town at 7:30 p.m.

John pulls into the parking lot, he sees Ellie's car and a woman standing beside it - it's Ellie dressed up in a way he's never seen before. Gone is the familiar college girl, replaced by a woman in tight black pants, a revealing black and red blouse, and black cowgirl boots.

Amused, John comments on her transformation and asks who her lucky date is for the night after their meeting. To his surprise, she reveals there is no one special in her life right now and that she simply wanted to dress her age for once - she's twenty-four after all.

John confidently offers to be Ellie's date for the meeting. She can't help but smile at his enthusiasm and takes his arm as they enter the restaurant. But her mood quickly changes when she spots Victor in a booth with a stunning woman. John discreetly points him out to Ellie, who is clearly bothered by his presence.

"Don't let him get to you," John advises, "that only gives him satisfaction."

Ellie begrudgingly agrees and they walk past Victor's booth, exchanging polite nods with him. Once they are seated, John suggests the buffet, which he knows Ellie always enjoys. They place their order and continue on their way, with John even greeting Victor's date along the way.

"Who was that?" Kai asks Victor.

"That's John Smith," Victor responds, "ever since he bought the old Stellar place, strange things have been happening there.

"What kind of strange things?" Kai inquires.

Victor proceeds to tell her about the dead girl's body found in the cave and the recent discovery of a young man. He mentions that after news of the girl's death broke, people began reporting strange creatures and ghosts in the area, causing many to trespass on the property in search of evidence.

Immediately, Kai realizes that Victor is the person she needs to talk to. She shares with him her vision when she was in a coma and how it led her to Beaver Creek. She also mentions the woman in black who visited her during her coma.

Victor remains expressionless and his face turns pale. Kai asks if he is okay.

"What was her name?" he asks. Kai tells him it was Mona.

Victor leans back in his seat and lowers his head, placing his hands on the table as if he is frustrated. Kai asks, what is wrong and why he is upset.

"Mona is my mother," Victor reveals.

Kai's mouth falls open in disbelief as she tries to process everything she has experienced and now learned. She can't believe that this woman could possibly be his mother.

"No way, it couldn't be the same woman. There's just no possible way," she says incredulously.

"She wanted you to find me, he says, because you have a very important piece of her. That piece is the key to bringing her back." Kai is confused, so he starts from the beginning.

"My mother was from Romania. She traveled through Europe until she reached the United States and found her coven and family in Salem, Massachusetts in the early 1800s. In case you were wondering, she was both a gypsy and a witch, while my father was an American Indian. I was born after she arrived here, and it was believed that my father had been killed, but his body was never found. Rumor has it that he is still alive and works as a healer. Many of our family members were burned during the Salem Witch Trials and afterwards. To survive, they split up and scattered throughout the country, blending in with the general population. Some became gypsies, others joined the military or worked in government positions to help protect our kind from persecution. My mother brought us here after my father disappeared, and we lived in the Stellar house for a while. One day, years later, a marshal found me working on a farm outside of town. He said I was the son of a witch and a gypsy, and that practicing witchcraft was illegal in Beaver Creek. They arrested me and tied me up. The short version of this story is that I was burned at the stake, and about a year later, the marshal killed my mother by cutting her into pieces and burying her in different locations to prevent her from coming back as a ghost or a stronger witch."

Kai reaches over and takes Victor's hands. "I understand your pain. My ancestors also suffered greatly like yours did."

Ellie and John finish their dinner a few booths down, and Ellie is eager to share her findings from the library with him. She explains that she discovered all the people involved in the killing of the Stellar family were eventually killed themselves, along with their family members. This pattern has continued up until present day. She also reveals that the girl's body found in the cave was a descendant of one of the original marshals responsible for killing the Stellar's.

John is astounded by this new information and his mind races with various theories. Could the black figure be George Stellar seeking revenge? He wonders if Benny Saxon, living in the caves for years, could be responsible for the creature sightings. Ellie admits she hasn't connected that piece yet but believes it could be a possibility.

She mentions wanting to interview Abigail Flynn's parents to gather more information on their relationship to the Marshals and deputies. Maybe that will help solve the mystery of these ongoing killings. But how do they stop George if it is indeed him?

Ellie then asks John a personal question about why his wife doesn't join him on these research trips. John explains that Lizzie is busy running their business and taking care of their sons back in Colorado. However, she recently called him and plans to visit with their boys soon. Their oldest son has been struggling in school and got into some trouble with a bad crowd, so Lizzie thought a change of scenery would do him good.

Ellie forces a smile onto her face, but inside she can feel a hint of jealousy bubbling up as she thinks about John's wife coming to visit. She worries that his wife might want him to leave and go back home, or even worse, demand that he quit his job.

"You'll have to introduce me to her sometime," she says half-heartedly.

"Definitely. Maybe we can all get together for a barbecue when she arrives," John responds with enthusiasm.

"That sounds great," Ellie replies, trying to hide any disappointment in her voice.

As they walk to her car, John remembers to give her the money for the week. She takes it and gives him a quick kiss on the cheek before driving off. "

Well that was unexpected and a bit not necessary. Kids these days."

John says getting in his truck.

# 27
## "MONA 1881"

DEEP in the depths of a cave beneath Sulfur Mountain, Mona prepares for an ancient healing ritual. She arranges a bed of straw on a flat granite rock and places the badly burned body upon it. Gathering all the necessary herbs and items, she carefully lays them on the rock with the body. She looks down at her son's unrecognizable form, she sets to work rubbing an enchanted herbal mud preparation over his entire body.

Using the powers of nature - water, earth, air, and fire - Mona calls upon their forces to aid her in healing her son. A gentle breeze begins to blow, carrying scents of walnuts, maple, and hickory. In its midst, a yellow light sparkles like glitter and is soon joined by a bluish white light that swirls around her. Raising her arms in supplication, Mona tilts her head back and gazes up at the ceiling of the cave as if seeking guidance from above.

The wind begins to swirl faster and faster until it gathers above Mona and shoots into her open mouth like a bolt of lightning. Her head falls forward and her eyes turn white as another force seems to take control of her body.

Mona walks over to the body covered in enchanted mud and moves her hands back and forth just above it. With the darkness of midnight and a full moon outside, the mud begins to writhe and ripple on top of the burnt flesh.

Speaking commands in her native Romanian tongue, Mona can feel warmth emanating from her hands as she continues moving them over the body.

As she continues to chant and sway, she feels the presence of other forces gathering around her in the cave. The spirits of the American Indian clan begin to encircle her and the body of mud, joining in on the chanting.

The energy in the cave intensifies as their powers unite. Suddenly, she feels a jolt as the energy collides within her. Her heart starts beating faster and faster, almost like a rabbit's heart, which is much faster than a humans.

With this surge of energy, the mud covering the burnt body begins to break apart, resembling millions of tiny worms moving over the flesh. In one swift motion, they burrow into the skin and the body starts convulsing.

Mona places her hands on different points of the body - one on the forehead and one just below the stomach area, where there is believed to be a meridian point for energy flow. She presses down firmly, a blue light glows from her left hand while a yellow light shines from her right hand. The energy from the other body is being drawn into hers as she channels it.

While Mona watches the burnt body calm down, a halo of white light forms all around the body. The light moves slowly like a wave over the feet, legs and up towards the torso and head. At the same time, a similar wave of yellow glittering light emerges from its head and travels down to its torso. When they meet in the middle, they clash with each other like a ball of energy and lightning striking a tree. This force is so strong that it breaks Mona's grip on the body and pushes her backwards. The energy has cocooned the body completely.

As she breaks off her connection with the American Indian spirits, they disappear into a white smoke. To ensure no evil spirits enter during this healing process, Mona places salt around the granite in a protective circle.

The energy starts to change to a soft, glowing light encapsulates the body with a yellow-blue edge circling the cocoon. From within, a bright white light of energy emerges and radiates outward. It's so bright that Mona can barely look at it.

Mona watches as her son's body is miraculously healed, the burnt and dead flesh falling away to make room for new, healthy tissue. The process takes hours, days even, but she stays by his side in the cave, exhausted but determined to see him fully restored. She falls into a deep sleep on the straw bed she had made for him before he died.

A gentle touch awakens her, and she sees her son squatting next to her. Tears well up in her eyes as she reaches out to touch his face, now fully human again. He lifts her onto the granite slab and places his hands on her head and stomach, chanting a healing spell in a language she doesn't recognize. She passes out from weakness.

Ancient Moons, lend your power.
Bring me peace this very hour. I call upon your strength & might.
I need your force of light to heal this body.
Bless this spirit on this sacred night.

Her son's hands radiate energy as he presses them deeper into her body and continues chanting. Suddenly, she gasps for air as blue smoke pours out of his mouth and enters hers. She coughs and chokes before passing out again. He removes his hands and caresses her cheek as she slowly opens her eyes.

Mona looks around the cave and sees her son standing over her - tall, handsome, with dark hair and yellow eyes. She reaches out to hug him and exclaims, "Victor, you're alive!"

# 28

"HURLEY"

AFTER DINNER WITH ELLIE, John parks his car in the garage and notices that Hurley is not there to greet him. He must be out running in the woods, John assumes. But as he walks to the edge of the driveway facing the field, its dark and almost eleven p.m. John strains his ears to listen for any sounds of Hurley, but all he can hear are the nocturnal creatures singing their songs - whippoorwills, crickets, and owls.

"Where could he be?" John calls out Hurley's name, but there is no response. Panicked, he calls out again and listens intently for any sign of his beloved dog.

Getting into his mule vehicle, John heads towards the creek, thinking that Hurley might have gone after some beavers or taken a swim in the water. However, a feeling of uneasiness grips John as he drives down the trail towards the creek. He pulls up to it, he notices that the water is flowing rapidly and has risen significantly. This must be due to heavy rains up north, causing the water to flow this way.

John calls out for Hurley, but all he can hear is the deafening sound of water rushing down the creek. He decides to continue up the creek in hopes of finding his missing dog.

Worried that Hurley may have been swept away by the current, John takes a spotlight from the mule and shines it through the woods and into the creek. He follows the beam of light as far as he can, but doesn't see anything.

Thinking that Hurley may have gone after an animal across the nearby field, John's heart sinks with dread. "Devil's Attic!" he exclaims, knowing it is a dangerous area.

He quickly drives the mule towards the field, then jumps out and rushes through the trees with a flashlight, calling for Hurley.

"Hurley! Come on, boy! Let's go for a run!" John desperately listens for any sign of his beloved dog - a bark, a whine - anything to let him know where he is.

He nears Devil's Attic, John's chest tightens with fear. He hesitates to call out again, afraid that he may hear Hurley trapped down there and know it would be nearly impossible to rescue him.

"Hurley? Are you down there?" John listens intently, hoping for a response. "Come on, boy. Let's go."

John stops in his tracks, straining to hear over the roars of the wind and the rustling of trees. He shouts for Hurley once more, his voice barely audible in the storm that is approaching. But then he hears something faint - it could be Hurley's voice, or is it a humming sound? As he listens closely, John realizes it's a woman humming a melody. Who could possibly be out here in this weather? Could it be that lady with long black hair or maybe someone lost in the cave?

The sound echoes through the cave, making it hard for John to determine its origin. Is it getting closer or farther away? It sounds like the woman might be in a tunnel. But it doesn't seem to be coming from inside Devil's Attic. It could be coming from somewhere else entirely. Still no sign or sound of Hurley.

Feeling a sense of dread, John walks back to where he left their mule. He can't bear to think that something has happened to his best friend, his companion. They have grown so close during their time together. Hurley has been instrumental in helping John with all the tasks on their land. Pulling up to the garage with a heavy heart, John takes a seat at the edge of the garage and listens for any signs of his best friend.

As he sits watching the last of the rain become a light drizzle, John hears the distant yipping of coyotes on the other side of

Sulfur Mountain. In that moment, he hums the same melody he heard coming from inside the cave.

A strong desire wells up inside him to go back into the cave by the creek. Suddenly, he feels a soft whisper in his ear saying, "I'm waiting for you." John jolts awake, realizing he had dozed off. The sun is rising over Sulfur Mountain, marking the arrival of fall as the leaves start to change colors . Everything is breathtaking, but then he remembers - Hurley never came back home.

Feeling anxious and exhausted, he steps into the steaming shower. After a refreshing rinse and a couple cups of hot coffee, his phone rings. It's Sheriff Taylor. John answers and immediately the sheriff can hear the distress in his voice. He asks if everything is alright. John explains that Hurley didn't come home last night and he's worried sick. The sheriff sympathizes with him and offers to come help search for Hurley.

Waiting for the sheriff, John decides to mow the grass around the garage. By 11:30 a.m., the sheriff arrives, and they quickly hop on the two-seater mule and head towards the creek. On the way, the sheriff asks if John has explored the cave yet. John replies no, that the creek was too fast and high when he attempted it before. He goes on to tell the sheriff about hearing strange noises in Devil's Attic.

"It started as a faint whine, but then it became more distinct - a woman humming. And then something weird happened," he explains to the sheriff.

"I felt this strong urge to go back out there, like someone was pulling me from inside." He admits that he had to fight against this overwhelming desire to find this mysterious woman calling out to him. The sound of her voice is still stuck in his head.

John tries his best to hum the tune for the sheriff, but it falls short of what he heard in Devil's Attic.

The sheriff seems skeptical as John shares these details with him. He suggests that it could be a siren - one of those creatures from books who use their beautiful voices and harps to lure sailors to shore so they can eat them alive. John laughs at this idea.

"I know it sounds crazy," he says, "but I'm certain it was a woman and I've never felt such intense desire in my life."

As they approach the creek near Devil's Attic, John notices that the water level has gone down, and they should be able to cross it. They take a deep breath and wade through the thigh-deep water, with the sheriff shouting out to John from behind.

"I'm glad you brought an extra pair of waders. If not, I'd be stuck waiting in the mule for you."

"I bought a couple pairs just in case we needed to cross the creek when it was deeper than usual. They are great to have."

As they enter the cave, they turn on their flashlights and continue deeper. The sheriff asks John if he checked the SD cards from the cameras yet. John explains that he has been busy and with Hurley gone missing, he hasn't had a chance. Deciding to stop and check for any photos, John inspects each camera as they move further into the cave.

Calling for Hurley, John thinks he hears him whimpering. Sheriff Taylor notices dog prints in the mud on the cave floor and points them out to John. He suspects that there is a human with Hurley, as evidenced by footprints next to the dog's tracks.

"This print looks small, probably a woman's," Sheriff Taylor comments.

"I think that's Hurley whimpering! He knows we're coming." John exclaims.

As they enter a large room in the cave, they scan their flashlights around looking for Hurley. Suddenly, the sheriff spots two sets of eyes staring back at them from across the cave.

"John! Over here!" He shouts.

John rushes over to join the sheriff and shines his light towards where the sheriff is pointing. They see two sets of eyes in the corner of the cave. John calls out for Hurley again and this time can hear him barking frantically, like he's scared or in danger. They hear a splash from what seems like something falling into water. Sheriff Taylor shines his light to the right and catches a glimpse of something diving into a pond within the cave.

"Did you see that?" He asks John.

"No, I didn't see anything."

"It looked like a large fish tail or some sort of reptile. It's the same one I saw before in here."

John sweeps his light around and finds Hurley lying on rocks across the pond. The sheriff explains that he will have to swim over to Hurley and coax him back to their side.

John keeps a watchful eye on Hurley as the flashlights shine on him. He can sense something isn't right, but he needs to get closer to be sure.

John passes his flashlight to the sheriff and removes his wading pants and shoes. He instructs the sheriff to keep the lights on Hurley while he swims over to him. Hurley struggles to reach John, stretching his neck out as he paddles towards him.

Once John reaches the rocks, he tries to help Hurley up, but he won't budge. John carefully examines Hurley, searching for any signs of injury. Suddenly, Hurley yelps and wags his tail as if apologizing for crying out. John informs the sheriff that it appears Hurley may have hurt his hind legs or hips.

Not knowing how to extract Hurley from the cave, John comes up with a plan. He swims back to the sheriff and directs him to retrieve some rope, a harness, and a bag labeled climbing gear from the garage. He also asks for extra camping lights to aid in visibility. John explains his plan: using rope anchored to opposite walls of the cave, he will create a hoist and slip Hurley into a harness before lifting him and transferring him over to the sheriff. The sheriff agrees and waits for John's return to Hurley.

Meanwhile, John comforts Hurley and lets him know everything will be okay. He is grateful to have found him alive. Suddenly, John hears the humming noise again. Hurley's ears perk up as if recognizing the source. But then it stops abruptly. A moment later, there is a splash in the water and the woman's humming returns, this time closer.

Straining his eyes in the dim light, John desperately wishes he had a flashlight with him. Meanwhile, he sees the beam of flashlights from shore shining towards him and the cave.

Curious about what could be lurking in the dark cave with them, John calls out, "Hello, is anyone there?" But there is no response to his call, and the humming noise that was plaguing them earlier suddenly stops.

Hurley starts wagging his tail again and even looks over the ledge of the rock towards the water. John notices air bubbles popping on the surface of the water through the dim light of the flash light from the shore. Hurley lets out a small whine, almost as if he is waiting for someone familiar to emerge from the depths.

"What's down there, Hurley? Do you know who it is?" John asks his furry friend.

Hurley looks up at John and wags his tail excitedly, as if to say yes. Just then, they see Sheriff Taylor's light shining through the cave entrance. With a rope in hand, the sheriff throws it towards John, and he quickly swims over to grab hold of it before it sinks. They both anchor the rope to the wall using some hooks and fasten a harness to it. With one end secured on each side of the cave, Sheriff Taylor slides the harness down the rope as hard as he can to reach John.

John grabs hold of the harness and takes it apart before wrapping it around Hurley. He gently lifts Hurley up and swims back towards Sheriff Taylor, slowly dragging Hurley along with him. Once they are reunited with the sheriff, they remove the harness from Hurley and decide that he will have to be carried back to safety on the mule.

As they quickly make their way out of the cave, John rides in the back with Hurley while Sheriff Taylor drives them back to their camper. The sheriff mentions knowing a good veterinarian in town and quickly calls him for assistance. As they load Hurley into John's truck, Sheriff Taylor informs him that Dr. Blair is expecting them across from Monticello Motel.

"I know where that is," John replies anxiously as he speeds off towards the motel.

John rushes to the Monticello Veterinarian clinic, he walks in and signs the paper and tells the girl that he was told to come here by Sheriff Taylor.

"Let me get you in room 1 and the Doctor will be with you as soon as possible."

"Thank you."

John cares Hurley into the room and puts him on the floor. Dr. Blair comes in and tells him he'll have to have some x-rays and then he will let John know what they find.

"It may take about an hour before I can get him into get x-rays. Do you mind leaving him here and we will call you when we are done?"

"That's fine. I'll be right back Hurley boy."

John goes out to his truck and decides to go get something to eat as he waits for the Vet to call. Heading to the Monticello Pizza place just down the street.

John just gets his lasagna when the phone rings.

"Hello, yes this is John, ok great that is good news. I'll be there in fifteen minutes to pick him up."

John asks the waitress if he can get his meal to go he has to leave.

Rushing into the vets office the girl informs him that Hurley has nothing broken he is just exhausted and possibly has pulled some muscles. The doctor prescribed some muscle relaxers for him to take for a few days. If his condition gets worse to call them immediately.

# 29

## "THE PROPERTY"

THE SCENT of freshly brewed coffee seeps into Kai's dream, causing her to stir. She is in shifted form, running through a dark forest when the aroma catches her attention and pulls her out of her dream.

As she comes to full consciousness, Kai realizes that the smell was not part of her dream, but from the real world. She reaches out to where her partner Victor usually sleeps but finds an empty space instead.

"Where did he go?" Kai mumbles as she scans the motel room in confusion. Maybe he's in the shower?

She throws off the covers and gets out of bed, helping herself to a cup of coffee. The room is quiet; the TV is off and there are no lights on besides the sunlight filtering through a small gap in the curtains. As she takes a sip of her coffee, she notices a note on the counter next to the coffee pot.

*"Good morning, sunshine! Enjoy your coffee and have a beautiful day."* Talk to you soon, my love, V

Beside the note lies a small bouquet of wildflowers. Victor carefully picks them up and places them in a cup, filling it halfway with water. The vibrant colors and thoughtful gesture from Victor bring a smile to her face.

She checks the time and realizes it's already seven in the morning. Kai quickly gets ready, making a mental checklist of all the tasks she needs to accomplish today.

"Today I'm going to that property and talk to this John Smith to see if he will let me take a look," she says to herself as she loads her car with her laptop and research materials.

Suddenly, she hears the screeching of tires across the street. Curiosity getting the best of her, Kai turns to see what's happening and notices a man jumping out of his truck and rushing into the vet's office with a dog in his arms.

"That looks like John Smith." Kai says aloud.

Observing from the motel parking lot, Kai decides to walk over and ask John about visiting his property. It may not be the best timing, but it's why she came here, besides finding Victor. As she approaches the vet's office, Kai sits down on a bench outside to wait for John to come out.

Just as she takes out her phone, it begins to ring - her boss Mr. Marcum checking in on her well-being. Kai reassures him that she is feeling much better after taking some time off to recover and asks if she can extend her leave by another two weeks. Mr. Marcum agrees without hesitation, pleased that she is taking care of herself. Kai explains that she is currently in Kentucky doing research on the finger bone that made her ill. Her boss approves of this idea and suggests that she write a field report on it to present at their next meeting when she returns to Virginia. This way, they can compensate her for her work instead of using up all of her vacation time.

John exits the vet's office and walks down the street. Kai spots him as she hangs up her phone and approaches him.

"Excuse me, sir? Can I have a moment of your time?" John looks at her in surprise.

"You were at the Chinese restaurant the other night with Victor," he says.

"Yes, sir. My name is Kai Liu and I work as a forensic technician at the lab in Quantico, Virginia. We processed the bone you sent for examination."

"That's quite a distance from here. What brings you down this way?" John asks.

"I actually came to find you and see if I could access the area where you found the bone," Kai explains.

"No problem, how about we meet up around 1:00 pm today, I have to wait on my dog Hurley he hurt his leg I believe." John says

"Oh dear I hope he will be ok? And no problem I will meet you there around 1:00 pm."

Kai decides to go get some early lunch from Nell's since it's nearly 11 in the morning. While at Nell's she puts John's address in the maps app and pin the location.

Once she's back in her car she clicks on the map app and follows the directions to John's.

"This is a beautiful place," Kai remarks as she arrives.

"Yes ma'am it is. Let me grab my mule so we can drive to the most active areas," John responds.

Kai hops into the passenger seat and they make their way across the field to where the young man's body was discovered. The crime scene tape is still standing, but Kai steps over it and places her hand just above the ground. Suddenly, she feels an intense tingle throughout her body, like electricity or energy surging through her. In an instant, it turns dark outside, and she sees a woman with long black hair standing over a man's body. The woman peers down at the motionless figure on the ground before turning around and walking away towards the tree line. Just then, she quickly looks back at Kai with fiery red eyes before vanishing into thin air. Kai stands up abruptly in shock.

Kai lets out a surprised exclamation, prompting John to ask if she felt something. She confirms, explaining that she had a vision of a woman with long black hair standing over a young man on the ground, which is eerily familiar to her. They get into the mule and make their way towards the creek, where John suggests they visit the old Stellar foundation.

Kai remembers it's where he found the finger bone and mentions that she has been drawn to this place since waking up from her coma. She reveals that she has been having visions of a woman named Mona who wants her to find something, but she doesn't know what it is yet.

As they ride through the fields towards the logging trail, Kai suddenly feels hot and starts sweating profusely, trying hard to resist the urge to shift in front of a stranger. When they arrive at the creek, Kai asks John if he hears chanting, but he only hears the sound of water flowing. Kai explains that she can hear screams mixed in with the chanting and covers her ears in an attempt to drown out the disturbing sounds. Concerned, John asks what's wrong and Kai leads him to the old foundation where she suddenly enters a trance-like state as the chanting and screams come to an abrupt stop.

As she kneels to touch the ground, a voice speaking in a Native American language catches her attention. She looks around and sees a traditional warrior on the edge of the creek. Suddenly, the surroundings transform before her eyes. A teepee's appears on the nearby hill, while children splash in the water below. Two white girls are playing with them, and in the distance, she can smell the aroma of pine and burning sage. The scent takes her back to her childhood, visiting her grandparent's home on the reservation. As she looks around, she sees native women tanning hides and grinding corn. The sound of the warrior's voice still echoes in the background, growing louder as he repeats his warning about an impending danger.

The sky darkens as the wind howls through the trees. The scenery rapidly transitions through different seasons - trees sprouting and growing, the creek shrinking to a dry patch of dirt, people and animals moving quickly through the woods. On a ledge above the creek, four silhouettes on horseback gaze down at the Stellar family's home. Faint screams can be heard, growing louder and more intense by the second. Kai can't bear it any longer; she drops down on her legs and covers her ears in an attempt to block out the noise. John rushes over, asking if she is okay as he tries to calm her down. Kai collapses onto her back, unconscious from the overwhelming chaos around her. John picks her up and carries her back to the mule and heads back to the camper as fast as he can. He lays her down on the couch and tries to wake her up, but she remains unresponsive.

Feeling unsure of what steps to take, John immediately calls the sheriff while he calmly places a cool cloth on her forehead.

"Sheriff that woman Kai came out and we where down by the old Stellar foundation and suddenly she went to her knees put her hands over her ears and fell backwards on the ground passed out. Yes, I have her on the couch in the camper right now. Ok I'll wait for you." John hangs up the phone.

John hears a phone ring briefly, he realizes the ringing phone is not his but Kai's, which must be in her pocket. It starts to ring again. After hesitating for a moment, he decides to answer it since Kai and Victor were together earlier and seemed friendly. Reluctantly, he answers the call.

"Hello, Victor."

"Who is this?"

"This is John Smith. Before you question why I'm answering Kai's phone, please hear me out. She came to my property this afternoon and while she was down by the creek, something happened, and she passed out. I've called the sheriff and he's on his way."

"Is she okay? Where is she?"

"She's here in my camper. I put her on the couch with a cold cloth on her head."

"I'll be there in fifteen minutes." Victor hangs up the phone.

As soon as the call ends, John hears a car door slam outside. He goes to investigate and finds Sheriff Taylor rushing towards them. John brings him into the camper where Kai is resting. Kneeling next to her, the sheriff asks if she fell and hit her head. John explains that she was kneeling when she fainted.

"Check if you have any smelling salts in your first aid kit," the sheriff instructs John.

John scrambles through the kitchen cabinet in the garage and finds a small packet in a first aid kit. He rushes back to the sheriff, holding it out for him.

"I hope this is still usable," he says with concern. The sheriff tears open the pack and holds it up near Kai's nose. After a few moments, she stirs and reaches up to push it away.

"What happened? And what's that smell?" She asks groggily. Just then, they hear a car pulling up outside and someone getting out of it.

"It must be Victor," John says, walking over to the camper door and opening it. Victor quickly enters and goes straight to Kai's side.

"Are you okay?" He asks, his expression full of worry.

She nods weakly and asks him why he's here. He explains that when he called her phone, John had answered and told him what happened.

Sheriff Taylor asks her what she remembers, and she tells them about the screams, chanting, and a member of one of the tribes warning her repeatedly that "the evil ones are coming."

"I think he was trying to warn me. Everything was like a fast-forward movie - the seasons changing, the landscape shifting, time itself rushing by," she recounts. "That's all I remember."

"Do you want to go to the hospital and get checked out?" The sheriff offers.

"No!" Victor immediately protests. "No! She'll be fine; she just passed out."

But Kai insists on going to get checked out, citing similar incidents since waking from her coma. The sheriff looks at Victor and then John.

"I'll take Kai to the hospital and have her checked out." Victor says.

"Well, I guess I'll be heading out then, let me know how everything turns out at the hospital Victor."

"One sec, let me check with John if he's okay with me setting up camp down by the creek."

Kai requests permission from John, and Victor expresses his disapproval.

He suggests that she should rest at the motel instead of in a tent. However, John offers them a large canvas enclosure which they use for hunting trips. It is 12' by 16' and has a fold-up kitchen complete with sink, stove, table, and chairs. Kai could stay there and continue her research. If she needs to shower, she can also use the facilities in the garage where there's and extra bathroom.

"That sounds perfect. Thank you so much." Kai says.

Victor tries to persuade her to stay at the motel, but she stands her ground and insists on staying in the enclosure. Victor then asks John if he would mind if he stayed as well to keep an eye on her. John agrees it's a good idea and offers them use of their 4x4 ATV to move around the property.

# 30

## "LILY"

VICTOR AND KAI get back to the motel around 8:00 pm and are exhausted. They decide to sleep and get a fresh start in the morning to set up camp by the creek on John's property.

"Hi good morning John. Thanks again for letting me here and do my research. I greatly appreciate it." Kai says.

"Oh, no problem. I hope you can answer the questions of why there's so many creatures and spirit animals around the property."

"That is one of my tasks to complete." Kai replies.

They transfer all their camping equipment onto the mule and drive over to the creek with John while Victor follows on the ATV. Once they arrive, John helps them set everything up and leaves them a cooler filled with ice, food, and drinks for the night.

As the sun begins to set, Kai and Victor settle by the creek. It's been a quiet evening so far, with no voices disturbing their peace. Kai is eager to explore the nearby cave, but Victor seems distant and out of sorts. When she asks him what's wrong, he brushes her off and says he just doesn't feel like himself. He can't shake the feeling that something is trying to communicate with him.

"I didn't sense or feel anything today," Kai comments as they sit around the flickering campfire.

Victor remains silent, fixated on the flames in front of him. Kai comforts him by rubbing his back and apologizing for not asking him to join her there. Still, he continues to stare into the fire without speaking.

Finally, he breaks his silence, "I think I can bring her back. I have most of her bones now; I just need a few more. But if I focus hard enough, she will guide me towards them. You still have the finger bone, right? Do you have it with you?"

Kai reaches into the bag and pulls out the object, placing it in Victor's open hands. She instructs him to hold it tight and close his eyes, assuring him that a vision may come to him. Kai holds his hand in hers, willing her own visions to merge with his.

Victor mutters something about the power of the cave and the essences of the earth and spirits aiding them. Kai shushes him and tells him to focus on finding her. As she continues to hold his hand, she senses his body twitching and grasps onto his hand tighter, offering reassurance.

She sees a blurry landscape, as if peering through a frosted window. It feels like walking through a tunnel of these windows, until suddenly the middle comes into focus but the blurriness remains at the sides. Realizing she has entered Victor's vision, Kai feels a strange sensation pulling her forward, as if falling down a hole. She catches sight of a man wearing a long black trench coat and a large hat that obscures his face. She can't see him clearly, but she can sense an ominous presence emanating from him.

Kai watches as the figure moves, its arms made of thick black smoke reaching inside its coat to retrieve something. She strains to see what it is, and her stomach churns when she realizes it's a human skull.

With slow movements, the figure tucks the skull back into its coat and starts to rise up, locking eyes with Kai. She can feel the evil aura emanating from it, an entity filled with malice and darkness. The figure's eyes glow red, causing Kai to startle and stumble backwards, losing her grip on Victor's hands.

She wonders if he saw the same thing. It's terrifying to think about. She looks at Victor for reassurance, he appears calm.

Was she really in his vision or did she have one of her own? Shaken, she walks around the campfire, shaking her arms to relieve the tingling sensation that feels like electric shocks.

On the other side of the fire, she sees a ghostly white image standing behind Victor with a hand on his shoulder. It must be his mother. She must be guiding him towards where they need to find her body.

Suddenly, Kai hears whispering all around them in the woods. She looks around but doesn't see anyone. White streaks shoot past her, almost hitting her, while more whispers fill the air. They're coming from all directions, but she can't make out what direction they are coming from.

Fear overwhelms her, and she immediately drops to the ground, taking cover behind a nearby tree stump. From her hidden vantage point, she sees streaks of white darting around and hears laughter. These must be the spirits she's been warned about. They playfully chase each other around, completely unaware of her presence.

"This is what John was talking about. Their spirit animals." Kai mumbles softly.

One spirit flies close to her, almost touching her before suddenly stopping in midair. She stares at it in amazement as it hovers before her. It appears to be Native American in appearance, with an animal skin seamlessly melded into its body. This must be one of the legendary spirit animals. Its face is half human, half bear, and its eyes glow a mesmerizing gold color. Kai reaches out to touch it, but it quickly darts away.

Another spirit joins in the playful dance, twirling and spinning before coming to a stop in front of Kai. She hears a ghostly voice whisper her name.

"Kai...Kai..."

Unable to resist, she watches as it floats closer to her. This spirit has the form of a coyote, with yellow eyes that seem to look right through her. As a child growing up on the reservation, Grandpa Moon had told her stories about these spirit animals - good ones and bad ones. He always advised them to trust their instincts above all else.

As she observes the friendly nature of these spirits, she realizes that they must have the ability to communicate with humans. But how can she understand them? Suddenly, she feels someone tickling her from behind and becomes very still. Across the campfire, she sees Victor sleeping on the ground. Waiting for the spirit animal to come back around in front of her, she can't help but feel a sense of wonder and curiosity about these mystical creatures.

Floating in front of her, the creature's eyes are shut. It appears to be a fox spirit animal. As Kai gazes at it, she can't help but smile back as it opens its eyes. She is amazed by their beauty;

one is green and the other blue, just like hers when she transforms into her own fox form. Could this be one of my ancestors? She wonders. Its face is a perfect blend of fox and human features, with a human torso in the front and an animal body in the back. Kai recognizes that it is a female spirit animal.

"Gorgeous," Kai whispers to the creature.

In response, it creates a gentle breeze that blows across Kai's face as if thanking her. Then she hears it speak; "Osiyo" (Oh-sa(y)-yo), which means hello in Cherokee. Kai echoes the greeting back to her.

Out of the corner of her eye, Kai sees something strange happening. White fur ripples down her arm, accompanied by a warm tingle on her skin, until she is fully transformed into a white-furred creature with black claws that resemble a dog's claws.

A quick chill rushes back up through Kai and she transforms back to human form. The spirit animal gestures for Kai to follow, but she hesitates, unsure of what it wants from her. She hears it say, Come with me.

Kai glances over at Victor, who is fast asleep on the ground. The spirit animal reaches out and touches Kai's arm a bolt of white light flashes. Kai walks around the campfire and grabs a flashlight next Victor before following the spirit animal.

As they trek towards a cave entrance, more spirit animals join them along the way. Switching on her flashlight for better visibility, Kai notices that everything looks different; most colors appear muted and dull while some are still vibrant. Her sense of smell and hearing are also heightened. It must be because I'm in a different realm, she realizes, without questioning the strange occurrences. Instead, she continues to follow her spirit animal guide.

Walking through the cave, following the spirit animal, she hears a faint whistling noise. It sounds like a woman singing a beautiful melody. Curious, she enters a large room within the cave and shines her light around, revealing a big stone table in one corner.

"This is where my mother was brought back, and I will bring her back," echoes a voice through the cave.

Kai spins around, searching for its source, but finds nothing. She follows the spirit animal to a pool of clear water and hears a humming coming from the far corner.

Suddenly, there's a splash as if something has leaped into the water. She looks around but sees only darkness. Kai bends down to touch the water, she sees visions appear on its surface. Four shadowy figures are moving quickly through a forest, hunting, or searching for something. They move together as one, breaking off in different directions before rejoining the leader. With determination in their movements, they search every inch of the forest, running with urgency towards their goal.

As she peers closer, the dark figures come to a halt on a nearby cliff and look up, revealing their faces. "Werewolves?" she whispers in disbelief. But as she looks closer, she notices the tattoo of two H symbols resembling a swastika on one of their arms. These are not werewolves - they are Hellhounds. Their eyes glow red and their saliva drips from their mouths as they shift into four human forms. Kai has heard stories about them but never believed they were real, as only a handful of people in her tribe have claimed to see one.

The alpha male stands at the front with the other three behind him, each perfectly spaced to show their position of power. Kai gazes down at them and thinks about the evil reputation they hold. Suddenly, her animal spirit nudges her attention towards them.

"Is this what you wanted to show me? Is this what's been upsetting you?" Kai asks.

The spirit animal nods and touches her hand, allowing her to see what it wants her to know.

In an instant, Kai is transported to a forest where she sees various shape shifters hiding in fear. Then, four black figures with glowing red eyes approach, letting out terrifying sounds.

The other shifters run and hide, clearly being hunted by these menacing creatures. But for what purpose?

Kai hears the gentle sound of water trickling and looks down. She realizes that she has lost control of her vision and is now standing in front of a pool of water as something ripples toward her. Kai takes a step back and watches as a stunning woman swims up and pulls herself onto a nearby rock. With long red hair, pale skin, and a shapely body from the waist up, it's clear that she is not entirely human - her lower half resembles that of a fish with beautiful, shining aquamarine, dark blue, purple, and black colors adorning her tail fin.

"Are you a mermaid? A real mermaid?" Kai asks in astonishment.

The woman laughs before responding, "Yes, I am. My name is Lily."

"You're breathtaking! Are there more like you?" Kai can't help but inquire.

"Oh yes, there are many of us."

"I always thought mermaids only existed in the ocean. Actually, I didn't even know they were real." Kai admits.

Lily gracefully dives back into the water and swims closer to Kai. Suddenly, she emerges from the water again, this time as a human. Kai wonders how she transformed so quickly.

"It's just a simple shake," Lily explains with a smile. "You'll get used to it. You just need to practice."

Curious, Kai attempts to transform when a glowing effect envelops her body, and she becomes partially shifted.

"You, see? It's not that difficult, you just need to practice." Lily reassures her.

"We have been waiting for you for a long time, Kai," Lily says with a serious tone.

"What do you mean?" Kai asks, puzzled.

"We need a leader. Someone who can help us fight against the evil that is coming. The same evil you saw in the pond earlier. It's hunting all of us. But you have the talent, the heritage, and the ability to help us. You are a guardian of animals."

Kai gazes up at the animal spirit with uncertainty, but the creature smiles and winks back at her.

"Is this what you and the other spirit animals want me to do? But I am nobody. I don't possess the strength or ability to protect anyone. I am not like the other shape shifters."

"But you are strong, Kai. In fact, you are stronger than all of them because you have a power deep within that has yet to be unlocked. Powers that will help us defeat the evil that's been hunting us. You just need to discover and learn how to use it."

"I think you may have chosen the wrong person, Lily."

"No, Kai. You are the one we've been waiting for. The spirit animals have been watching you and they know your true heritage. They also know that you possess their powers - powers that will aid you in becoming more than just a fox shifter. You can transform into any creature you desire with ease. And this cave will guide you in finding that strength. That is why you are so important; you're our only hope."

"What kind of powers does this cave hold?" Kai asks Lily curiously.

"The powers of this cave are beyond your wildest dreams. They can bring death or everlasting life. In this cave, there is a balance of good and evil, and it is important to be cautious and to learn from the shifters and the creatures that inhabit the forests and caves. They have valuable lessons to teach you.

Kai lowers her gaze to the ground as she feels a spirit animal touch her back with a slight electric shock. She knows she must try for their sake; they have been waiting for her. Despite living in Virginia, she is determined not to let them down. But then she remembers her responsibilities at home and admits, "I can't stay here. I need to go back home."

"You will find that leaving will only make things worse. The visions, visits, and urge to return will become stronger. You will be drawn back here," Lily warns.

Kai realizes that Lily is right, deep down inside. She has noticed how easily she can shift around the property since she's been here. It's not as hard and she feels that the spirit animals are family from another era there to guid her and teach her to be stronger and help them. This is where she is meant to be and where she is needed.

"This is where I'm meant to be..."

# 31

## THE CONJURING

Footsteps echoes through the cave, causing Kai to spin around and shine her flashlight towards the entrance. A figure emerges from the darkness and approaches her slowly. In a panic, she turns back to where Lily and the spirit animal were just moments ago, but they are both gone. Where did they go?

"Who's there?" Kai calls out, her voice trembling slightly.

"It's me, Kai," the figure responds.

"Victor? What are you doing here?"

As he steps closer, Kai notices something different about him. His eyes have changed to a shimmering amber color.

"I had a dream about my mother," Victor explains. "She showed me how to find her and gather the necessary items for the ritual to bring her back. And now that I finally have access to this cave, I can finish what I've been planning for so long."

Kai senses a distant vibe from Victor and asks him what's wrong. He brushes off her concern, claiming that everything is fine. But she knows he's not telling her everything; she can sense it.

"There's a lot about me that you don't know," Victor admits. "I'm a War-Djinn - part warlock, part Jinni. I have powers that can do incredible things."

He reveals that he has been hiding his true identity as a normal person for far too long. But when Kai touched his mother's finger and the ring, it triggered something in him and unlocked his full potential. Now he can shift to any location she is in and only reveal himself when he chooses to. He used this power to make Kai believe she was dreaming when he was actually with her in physical form.

"I needed someone like you," Victor confesses. "Someone pure and full of light, to help me bring my mother back. That's why I've been following you, waiting for the right moment to reveal myself."

He strides past her and approaches the large granite slab in the center of the cave. With his head bowed, he places both hands firmly on the surface. She can see the strain in his muscles as he presses down with all his might.

Suddenly, he releases and holds his hands out in front of him as if holding an invisible ball. A bright yellow lightning bolt dances between his palms, eventually forming a reddish-orange sphere at its center.

She watches in awe as he makes the ball grow larger by moving his hands in a fluid, waving motion. Then, with a throwing gesture, he sends it shooting across the cave. Everywhere it passes, flames ignite from what look like bolts of lightning, illuminating torches and candles scattered throughout the cavern.

The sight is mesmerizing to her, and she can't help but feel a magical energy pulsing through the air. As she looks up, she sees white glowing objects swirling in spiral patterns high above them. Looking around, she notices intricate carvings on the walls and pillars that resemble those found in ancient Egyptian or Aztec temples.

"It's so beautiful," she whispers to herself, taking in the surreal scene before her. Just then, the white creatures descend upon her and begin circling around her in an otherworldly dance.

"Fairies?" she repeats in disbelief.

Glowing white creatures with dragonfly-like wings circle around her. They are as big a sparrow and each one has a human-like face with intricately braided hair adorned with various accents that match their eyes. One has leaves and flowers woven into her emerald, green locks, while another has puffs of cloud in her sky-blue hair and white eyes with black pupils. The third fairy's hair resembles waves of water and is decorated with shells, and she has the most vibrant blue eyes she's ever seen. The fourth one's hair is like flames, intertwining shades of yellow, orange, and red, and her fiery orange eyes have a bright yellow ring around them. The fifth fairy's hair contains stones like those found in the New Mexico desert, and her clay-red eyes are surrounded by a beautiful whitish-pink color.

Four of the fairy represents an element: earth, fire, water and air. The one seems to be the leader or the queen. They all have elf like ears on the sides of their heads and feathered torsos with human arms and legs.

How incredible, she thinks, observing these beings. As they fly past Kai, they emit a high-pitched buzzing noise and gaze at her with just as much curiosity as she has for them.

They land on a ledge near Victor and turn to face him. She follows them with her eyes before returning to the slab where she sees large granite columns standing at the sides like an entrance to a room. Why is everything changing? She wonders as she slowly walks around to the other side of the table.

Victor places his hands on the table and begins to address his family.

"Welcome, my dear relatives. We have a lot of work to accomplish in a short amount of time. I will need each of your assistance with this ritual."

He raises his hands and bones start to emerge from a bag lying on the floor and onto the table before him. With a flick of his wrist, they align themselves precisely as he desires. On the table lies a human body, missing an arm, hand, and head.

Kai feels a tingling sensation and a pull around her body. She tries to remain calm, not wanting Victor to see her fear. As she stands by his side, she suddenly feels something tugging at her pants. Startled, she watches as an evidence bag from her pocket floats out towards Victor. He takes out the finger bone with a ring attached and sets it down on the table. Making a motioning gesture with his hand, three fairies fly out of the cave while the rest stay perched on the ledge, silently observing every move Victor makes.

He begins to chant under his breath, causing Kai to cast furtive glances his way. She notices a shadow moving within the cave, accompanied by strange sounds resembling growls and scuffles as if it is fighting against something. The shadow draws closer to the slab where they stand. It appears to be that of a human figure, bound by ropes or some other object, being dragged towards them.

"Holy crap!" Kai exclaims.

"That looks just like the black figure in my vision before I entered this cave."

Victor turns to face the dark figure as red eyes materialize from within the swirling smoke that surrounds it. They appear like two blazing flames, squinting as they observe Victor's movements towards them. Despite its attempts to struggle against its restraints, it remains trapped. Victor approaches it directly and reaches inside its smoky form, retrieving a human skull. The black figure attempts to fight back, emitting a low moaning sound and displaying visible anger towards Victor's actions.

Kai lowers her head, unable to watch as Victor returns to the slab with the skull and places it in position. Soon after, the fairies return carrying something in their delicate hands. They gently place it on the table before Kai, revealing it to be the missing arm with one finger absent from the hand. As she watches, the bones begin to move and snap into place, forming a complete arm.

Kai can't believe what she is witnessing - true magic that she has only ever heard about in cautionary tales told by the elders. Her fear intensifies as she realizes the power that lies within Victor and what he is capable of achieving.

She tries to calm herself down, but the warmth inside her keeps growing hotter and hotter. Sweat drips down her face and body as she watches Victor standing in front of the slab.

She feels weak and shaky as he looks at her with a blank expression. His hand moves in front of her, directing his movements towards her and making upward gestures. Looking back at the bones, she notices a shimmering glow down her arm and feels a tingling sensation accompanying it. She sees grayish white fur sprouting along the top of her arms and then spreading to her face and head. She realizes with horror that she is shifting without even trying; Victor must be controlling her transformation.

She examines her arms, noticing how thick with fur they are on the top but almost hairless underneath. Her hands now have thick fur on the back, reminiscent of a paw, but her fingers still have long black claws protruding from them.

Victor grabs her arm, causing her to jump in surprise. She looks at him briefly before averting her eyes to break contact. Her mother had warned her never to make eye contact with any shapeshifters or Skinwalkers; they could mimic your appearance and take over your body. Kai hesitates, not wanting to give in to Victor's control, but he tightens his grip until she is forced to move closer to him.

He reaches into his pocket and pulls out a small dagger. Squeezing Kai's wrist until her hand opens, he cuts a slice in the palm of her hand. Despite holding back any words or expressions of fear, she can't help but let out a sound like an injured animal.

Victor continues without breaking his concentration, turning her hand over and placing it above the mouth of the skull on the slab. He squeezes harder until blood flows from her hand and into the mouth of the skull.

Kai's body tenses up, but Victor tightens his grip on her arm to keep it above the skull's mouth. His eyes are glowing a fiery yellow orange as he smirks at her and let's go of her hand. She cradles it under her other arm in pain and steps away from him. He begins to chant into the darkness,

*I summon now, from the dark night*
*The spirits of earth, water, fire, and sky*
*Bestow upon me their healing might*
*To revive this lifeless sight*
*Give breath to this final hour*
*And raise this corpse with your blazing power*

Something stirs within the cave. Kai squints and sees a small stream of mud slowly approaching them. It crawls up two steps onto the floor and creeps along the rock towards the granite slab. The mud coats the human bones resting on the slab. A brilliant white light emerges from the mud, growing higher and higher until it hovers about two foot above the bones.

Streaks of white lightning zip through the whitish fog like capsuling the bones. Kai and Victor, centered around the granite slab, she looks up and sees a swirling mist like substance as they move to the right.

Victor places his hands on the glowing cocoon surrounding the mud-covered bones. His eyes widen and his body jolts as if an electric current is coursing through him. Suddenly, his eyes turn a bright blue color, matching the outer glow emanating from the cocoon. Blue and white bolts of energy shoot out from where his hands touch, traveling all around the cocoon in a rhythmic dance as they move from head to feet.

The mud starts bubbling and swirling faster and faster as the electric energy bolts increase in speed. Victor begins to shake, and Kai is unsure of what to do. She's afraid to touch him or say anything. The spirits continue their quick paced circle above the dark figure still trapped in the corner of the cave. Suddenly, Victor's hands are thrown off the cocoon and he nearly falls backwards, catching himself with a few stumbling steps.

His eyes emit a whitish glow as he gazes at her with a smile. She is frozen, unsure of what to do or think in this strange situation. Despite her attempts to shift back, she remains in her altered form, perhaps under some kind of spell from him. But maybe it's better this way; she heals faster and is stronger in this form.

Victor reaches into the glowing cocoon and scoops up a handful of mud with his fingers, gently placing it onto the wound he created on Kai's hand with his dagger. He holds her hand tightly between his own, causing a warm and slightly burning sensation that quickly fades away, leaving behind a coolness. When she looks down at her hand, she finds that it has completely healed, as if nothing had happened. Stunned, she rubs her hand with the other one while looking up at Victor in confusion.

Should I thank him? Smile at him? She wonders but remains silent.

The mud recedes from the bones and flows towards the feet slowly, revealing black hair underneath. Kai can't help but gasp in shock.

'What is that?' She mutters under her breath.

"Is that black hair?" Victor turns to look at her with an intense gaze that sparks anger within Kai. She immediately stops speaking and avoids eye contact.

The thick mud slowly oozes down the body, covering every inch of her skin before flowing off the edge of the slab and disappearing into the cave. Kai watches a woman lays on the slab, glowing with a beautiful shimmering light like something out of a fairy tale. With hair as dark as night and skin radiating with life, she looks almost like Sleeping Beauty.

As the light fades and retreats to its source, Victor places his hands on the woman's head. A gentle breeze begins to blow through the cave, stirring up a white mist that drifts towards them in waves. Kai feels fear rising within her as she watches this mysterious mist approach. She can feel it brushing against her face as it hovers above the woman's body on the slab.

Victor grabs Kai's hand and something else grabs her other hand. She turns to see that all the fairies have formed a circle around them, holding hands and pulling Victor towards them. As the mist descends into the woman's mouth, her body begins to convulse uncontrollably. Kai wants to help but finds herself trapped in the circle by an unbreakable grip from both Victor and the fairies.

Eventually, the convulsions stop, and the woman sits up on the slab, taking in deep gasps of air. Her eyes are pitch black with red-tinged whites, and she seems almost scared as she stares at the black figure standing before her.

She gestures towards the group of hands, causing them to break free from their circle and float upwards. Victor removes his shirt and drapes it over the woman's shoulders. Kai watches in shock as the woman floats towards a black figure.

They observe as the woman reaches into the black figure and tears out its heart. The figure thrashes and roars in pain, but the woman remains determined. She digs deeper, pulling out some sort of parasitic creature that writhes in her hand and screeches loudly. Kai gasps and asks what it is.

The woman walks over to a nearby slab of granite and inspects the creature. It resembles a large leech, roughly twelve inches long and seven or eight inches thick. The woman struggles to hold onto it as it squirms and tries to break free from her grasp.

"It's the malevolence that has kept this creature alive for so long. We must destroy it to ensure it never returns." He whispers into her ear, placing gentle kisses and nibbles along her neck. She leans into him, feeling a sense of safety in his embrace.

The woman carefully sets the black creature onto a table, watching as it squirms and writhes in her hand. She speaks incantations and spells, while Kai listens intently to her words.

*I banish you from this realm*
*Never again shall you show your face*
*I condemn you to eternal slumber*
*So, you may never harm another soul*
*I sever your limbs with this knife*
*As you once did to me in a past life*
*Darkness envelope this place*
*Wrap this cave in an embrace*

(All of the flames in the cave suddenly go out)

Ancient ones, hear my plea (Lightning bugs swarm into the cave, illuminating the space)

Destroy this creature from the depths of hell he came

Send him back to his rightful domain.

Together, they watch as she cuts the leech-like creature into pieces. The screams of its victims can be heard echoing through the cave, as if flying around in the air. With each slice, crackling electricity dances across the woman's fingers and over the dissected pieces of the parasite creature. The pieces writhe and crawl away, attempting to piece themselves back together and fight for survival.

The woman moves her hands in fluid motions, channeling more energy with each movement. Eventually, each piece of the parasite shrinks and melts until all that remains is a wax-like substance. She sets each piece on fire and watches as they burn to ash.

Kai turns to Victor and embraces him tightly, too afraid to run or say anything. A tingling sensation washes over her, trans-forming her back into a human. She wants to flee from the cave, but she is worried about what might happen if she does. In this moment, she trusts him completely as he holds her tight in his arms. He kisses her head and spins her around hugging her tightly.

"How am I going to survive without him?" she wonders.

"I want to be with him; he is my mate. I have never felt this way about anyone before...I am deeply in love with him." Tears threaten to spill from her eyes as she realizes the depth of her feelings for him.

"I love you, Victor," she whispers in his ear. He pulls away slightly to look into her eyes and responds with a forehead kiss. Placing his hands on her cheeks, he brings their foreheads together and says, "I love you too, Kai Moonfeather Liu, with all my heart."

Suddenly, a woman appears and moves towards them. Kai stays close to Victor, still holding onto him tightly. Without warning, something grabs her from behind and throws her away from him. She screams as she collides with the rocks and falls to the ground. Shocked by this turn of events, Victor instinctively strikes out at the woman who attacked Kai, throwing her backwards over the granite table.

"How dare you touch my mate!" he shouts.

Panicked, Victor rushes over to Kai's unconscious body and gently places her on the slab. He calls out to her, kissing her and stroking her cheek in an attempt to wake her up. As he places one hand between her hips, expecting the familiar burning tingling sensation that signifies she has transformed back into a human, he instead feels a cooling sensation.

"What have you done to her?" he demands.

"Victor, listen to me," his mother says sternly. "No woman is good enough for you."

"But she is..." Victor begins before his mother interrupts him.

"Victor, Victor!" Kai's voice cuts through the tension in the air.

"Who is this woman, Victor, and why is she so important to you?" his mother asks.

"She is the reason you are here right now," Victor responds, determined to protect Kai from any harm. "Don't hurt her again!"

Victor grasps Kai's hand tightly and presses his lips gently against her skin. Tears stream down his face as he continues to apologize. Kai reaches up and places a hand on his cheek. She can feel the rough texture of his unshaven beard beneath her fingers. He kisses her hand in return before helping her sit up. She moves her legs off the table and onto the floor with his assistance. Victor then positions himself between her legs, pulling her close to his chest.

"Victor, what happened?" Kai asks, still bewildered.

"This is my mother, Mona," Victor introduces, revealing a woman standing at the end of the granite slab.

"I am deeply sorry for my actions towards you, Kai. I wasn't aware of your identity. I had no control over myself and I beg for your forgiveness," Mona speaks sincerely to Kai.

"Yes, ma'am. You visited me while I was in a coma."

"That's right. I was trying to send you a message, but I wasn't sure if you were receiving it. You were quite ill during my last visit."

"We should leave before John comes looking for us. Mother, I need to take you back to my house and figure out how to explain this." Victor says.

I'll handle it, John. This is my research area." Kai interjects.

"You need to rest and recover from all that has happened. Come with me back to my house and let me take care of you. I'm worried about your head injury." Victor insists.

He helps Kai off the slab and when her feet touch the ground, she stumbles; he quickly catches her in his arms.

"See? I won't leave your side. You're coming home with us even if I have to carry you all the way to the car." Victor says determinedly as he picks her up in his arms.

They leave the cave and are greeted by the first light of dawn. The trees cast long shadows as they make their way across the creek. Victor sets Kai down and quickly gathers their belongings with Mona's help.

"Mother, you'll ride with us in the car. Please lay down in the back seat. I don't want John to see you yet." Victor instructs.

"Yes, Victor," Mona replies obediently.

They make their way back to the camper on the ATV, hoping John is still asleep. As they approach the closed garage doors, Kai's condition hasn't improved and Mona wonders what their next step should be.

Victor helps Kai off the ATV and carefully places her in the front seat of his car.

He opens the back door for Mona and she climbs in.

"Lie down on the seat, Mom," he whispers.

He walks around and starts the engine, making their way down the driveway towards his home on the other side of town.

# 32

## "THE ANSWERS"

AFTER RESTING at Victor's house as instructed by the ER doctor Kai is feeling much better. Despite a few scraps and bruises she decides to call John to schedule a meeting with the evidence she found from the camping trip on the property. Hoping Ellie's finding's might help answer questions they have been searching for.

She enters Nell's Diner, gathering her papers as she walks in.

"Hi, nice to see you," John greets her and shakes her hand.

"Sheriff Taylor, thank you for coming. I have some important information for you," Kai tells him.

"This is Ellie, my research assistant. She's a local from Beaver Creek and knows about all the missing persons throughout the years."

"It's great to meet you, Ellie."

"Likewise. I've heard a lot about you, Kai."

"I hope it was all good things," Kai replies with a smile.

"What happened to your eye?" John asks, noticing Kai's bruised cheek and black eye.

"I slipped in the cave the other night and hit my head on some rocks. I knocked myself out for a few minutes," Kai explains as she turns her head to hide the black eye.

"Now, let's get started."

They take their seats and Kai begins explaining Native American mythology. She reveals that for centuries, they have shared stories with children about shape shifters, skin walkers, and other strange creatures that live among us. Each country and each nationality have their own unique shape shifters who have the ability to transform into any animal at will. Most are only able to change between human form and one type of animal, depending on their DNA makeup. Many are born with these ability to shift into a few too many.

"Is it possible for someone to become a shape shifter if they don't have the DNA?" Ellie inquires.

"Yes, it can happen. Some shape shifters can transmit their DNA through biting or getting their blood into an open wound or ingestion. However, it's not as simple as it sounds; transferring the DNA to a normal human is tricky and often unsuccess-ful. It requires a significant amount of DNA from the shape shifter in peak transformation. The most successful method is taking a vial of blood during this time and injecting it into a normal human. The transformation process usually takes around 30-60 days, depending on the species of shape shifter. Sometimes it can take up to a few years for noticeable changes to occur.

"Will people know if they've been infected? Are there any signs?" Sheriff Taylor asks.

"Yes sir, there are moderate changes that occur. Their senses become heightened - they can smell things they couldn't before, hear better, and see with more clarity. They may even be able to spot shape shifters in their non-shifted forms using their sense of smell. Physical changes also occur, such as hair, eye color, facial features, and physique altering to match that of the shape shifter's shifted form. Another change is an increase in sex drive during certain lunar phases. As the full moon approaches, their desire burns stronger and satisfying it can be difficult without a willing partner who knows how to handle it. Otherwise, they may seek out another shape shifter to fulfill their urges, or worse they could find a human and well we know if they aren't willing what may happen."

"Interesting...sounds like material for an X-rated film." John adds with a laugh.

"After centuries of finding dead bodies, we finally found and destroyed the culprit. It was a large black figure known as a doppelgänger, capable of doubling themselves or taking on another body. The doppelgänger had been doubling a U.S. Marshal, who apparently possessed powerful witchcraft abilities. When the Marshal killed someone with this power, it would combine with the victim to create a powerful evil entity. This explains all the murders in Beaver Creek, which have been connected to the missing Marshal and his deputies. However, there is also a shapeshifter residing in the cave system inside Sulfur Mountain - a shape shifter named Lily who revealed herself as a mermaid."

Sheriff Taylor confirms having seen something jump into the water that could have been her.

"But there is still concern about another evil presence in the cave that Lily warned about, one that appears to be female and malevolent." Kia exclaims.

"That must be Mary Stellar," Ellie says with a hint of excitement.

"You mean all these years it's been Marshal Isaac Crane that was doing all these killings? Sheriff Taylor asks.

"Yes, sir he is the one that has been doing most of the killings since it all started in the later 1800's. Kai confirms.

"Yep. When I was a kid, my parents warned me not to go near the caves in Beaver Creek because of the creature that Mary Stellar had become. It was like an urban legend in this area. All the kids would dare each other to go into the caves," adds Ellie.

"I remember hearing this when I was growing up and now my kids talk about it too," Sheriff Taylor chimes in.

"But what if it's not just a story or an urban legend.? I mean the evidence we found tells a few different things about the few that never where found and killings of different degrees started after they went missing." Ellie raises an interesting point. Sheriff Taylor encourages Ellie to continue telling them about Mary Stellar.

"People say she still lives in those caves, coming out to seduce young men and suck the life from their bodies. Each soul she takes adds years to her own life. Curt was 21 when he died, but he could have lived until he was 80. That means 59 years were added to Mary's life by taking his. She typically goes for young men, but has been known to go for any male throughout history. She uses sexual desire to lure men away from others and they never come back. Sometimes they find the bodies sometimes they never do. I have a feeling she drags them into the cave system before she finishes them off. That's probably why we haven't seen anything like Curt before."

Ellie continues, "They say she was responsible for finding Benny Saxon when he went missing. He was rappelling down into the cave when he got cut on a sharp piece of rock and his rope broke. He fell to the bottom. As Christopher hoisted the rope up, he thought it had caught Benny, but Benny was unconscious from a blow to his head. The stench of blood in the cave drew Mary's attention towards him. It's a mystery why she didn't drain him of his life force like she did with others. Instead, according to legend, she took him back to her realm within the caverns and nursed him back to health. She fed him raw meat from animals possibly humans she hunted. It's possible she also used natural remedies found in the nearby forest and fields to heal him. That explains what April saw that night. In her vision, there was a woman carrying a young girl to this creature outside of Devil's Attic. It must have been Mary bringing food to Benny." Ellie concludes.

"You're right, Ellie. That must be what happened to that little girl who went missing when I was a child. My father worked on that case. I remember we couldn't go outside at night for weeks and no one could camp near Beaver Creek. Her body was never found. I think her name was Macy Coldwell, about 10 or 12 years old when she disappeared." Sheriff Taylor said.

"How did Mary become what she is?" Kai asks.

"After the Marshals took the girls, Mary managed to kick one of them and escape, leaving her younger sister Molly behind. Unfortunately, they did find Molly she was deceased. The deputies and Marshal Crane never confessed what happened to the girls once they had them in custody. They never found Mary or her remains until some hunters heard screams while out in the woods one day. They followed the cries until they came across a young girl with long black hair and torn dress on the ground with a black haired monster on top of her, biting her neck. The men shot at the creature, thinking it was Mary Stellar who had gone missing. But as they fired, it turned to face them with its glowing red eyes and massive bat-like wings unfolded from its back before flying off into the trees with Mary in tow. The forest was too dense to pursue it. When the men returned to town and told the Marshal what happened, he dismissed their story, thinking they were drunk and seeking the reward money. This is what I found in the old newspapers and talking to the town folks during my research." Ellie says.

The sheriff leans back in their chair, deep in thought as he reflects on the connection between all the stories and events that have taken place over the years.

"All these years and all the stories in my wildest dreams I'd never have put together all this information." Sheriff Taylor says.

"But if Mary was carried off by a black creature what was it? And is it still out there? I'd think this creature nursed Mary back to health as Mary did Benny. But still leaves the question what was the creature? And is this why Mary became this Succubus creature? Kai questions.

"It is a good possibility that is what Mary became is a succubus. As the story goes; A succubus or succubi is a female demon or supernatural entity in folklores who appears in dreams to seduce men. Usually through sexual activity. During this sexual event the succubus will drain or harm the man with whom she is having intercourse with." Ellie explains.

John asks about the destruction of the doppelgänger or black figure known as Marshal Crane. Kai assured him that it was vanquished with the assistance of Native spirit animals and some powerful magic. This leads John to realize that this must have been the entity that had been haunting the field at night by the old walnut tree.

"Those white streaks in your field at night are spirit animals and they are trying to communicate. They were trying to warn you of danger that was there and as they did for me they warned me of another threat that I believe is coming this way." Kai replies.

With everything coming together, they agree that they have found most of their answers, but are unsure of what to do with this crazy story. They decide to keep it an urban legend, especially since Mary and Benny Saxon are still out there and more people could potentially go missing.

As everyone discusses the situation, Ellie points out that Tori is likely Mary Stellar, given her resemblance to the description - long black hair, blue eyes, and a tendency to pursue men. The idea is met with laughter, but also serves as a reminder for John to be cautious around Tori in case she does come knocking on his camper door one night.

"I have one more thing to tell you," Kai says seriously.

"What is it?" Sheriff Taylor asks.

"I had a vision. Something is coming towards Beaver Creek. I can sense it."

"That's not crazy compared to everything else we've discussed," Sheriff Taylor replies calmly.

"There are four black dog-like creatures headed this way. They're hunting shape shifters and other creatures seeking refuge here on your land, John. They're evil - in mythology, they're known as the 'Hellhounds'. I saw a symbol on one of their arms - two 'H' letters tattooed on the top of their left arm, resembling a German swastika. If you see anyone with this symbol or any new people traveling in packs of four males, pay close attention. They'll most likely be young, late early twenties to early thirties. They'll be checking out schools, colleges, motels, and diners for suspected shape shifters." Kai explains.

"Is this what the spirit animals warned you about when you were in the cave?" Ellie asks.

"Yes I believe it is Ellie."

"Thank you for letting us know. We'll keep an eye out." John says earnestly.

"I'll do the same. In a small town like this, I usually come across new faces sooner or later. I like to know who's here." Sheriff Taylor adds.

"If there are no further questions, I think we're done here." Kai concludes.

"I believe we are gang. This was one of the most informative meetings I've attended." Sheriff Taylor adds.

They all stand up from the table and shake hands before making their way outside into the parking lot.

"Keep me informed on anything new." Sheriff Taylor tells them.

# 33

## "GOODBYE"

"BEFORE WE ALL leave I'd like to say this has been truly amazing. I am going to miss all of you, and I'd like to keep in touch with you all. Here is my card with my email and phone numbers on it. Please if you have found anything else John, Ellie, Sheriff call me." Kai says.

"Are you heading back to Virginia, Kai?" Sheriff Taylor asks.

"Yes, sir. I'm leaving this afternoon," Kai replies.

"Well, if you ever get tired of the FBI, I have an empty office that I'd love for you to fill as a criminal investigator for me."

"Wow, Sheriff Taylor, that's a tempting offer. Can I think about it and get back to you later? I have some things to take care of first."

"No problem, just come see me when you're back in town. You are coming back to visit, right?" He gives her a warm hug.

"You're going to make me cry, Sheriff," Kai says as she returns the hug.

"I guess it's my turn for goodbyes." John joins in on the hug with tears forming in his eyes.

"Thank you both for everything. You've been such amazing friends. It's going to be hard for me to stay away from this place." Kai wipes away her tears.

"John, your property is truly special. The spirit animals and shape shifters feel safe here. Please do everything you can to protect it and don't let them down."

"Don't worry, I will take care of them. And Kai, I'll reserve a cabin for you on the property."

"A cabin? What do you mean?" Kai asks.

"I'm building several small cabins for visitors on the east side of the property by the tree line. One will be specifically for you. You can come stay whenever you want or even live there if you come back. The shape shifters would love to have you here with them," John explains with a smile.

"I don't know what to say...thank you, John. It's going to be even harder to leave now."

After saying goodbye and giving hugs all around, they all go their separate ways. Kai is already packed and checked out of her motel room, ready for the long drive back to Virginia.

Victor is waiting for her at his house to say his goodbye. Kai pulls up in his driveway tears start forming in her eyes.

"This is going to be very hard to do." She says hanging her head before getting out of the car.

Walking up to the front door before she can ring the door bell it opens. Victor standing there with watery eyes. Kai sees him and burst into tears.

Victor grabs her and hugs her and she hugs him tight.

"You know you don't have to go baby really I beg you to stay."

"Honey I know and I really want to stay but I have so much to do back home before I can make that decision to move here. I hope you understand. I can't just walk away from my job I have to give proper notice, I have to give my landlord notice, I have to pack and...."

"I understand. And I'm willing to come and help you. Just say the words Kai. Ask me to come with you."

"You need to stay here and take care of things around here. You have a job, you have the answers to everything going on around here, John has his hands full so he will need help. Whether building the cabins, finding more creatures, helping any of them that need refuge. Honey you need to be here. I'll be back as soon as I can. Okay?"

Victor agrees and they hug but never say goodbye.

"I'll call you in a few hours to make sure everything is going good on your way back." Victor tells her as he shuts her car door.

"That sounds like a plan, if I get lonely or when I stop for gas I will call you to honey." Kai gives him one last kiss.

# 34

## "BENNY SAXON"

Mary Stellar, also known as Tori, found Benny Saxon the day he fell into the cave. She brought him into her realm within the caves, where she had made a comfortable home for herself. It was clear to her that Benny was young and injured, so she used her knowledge of herbal preparations to heal his broken ribs and arm. She also taught him how to navigate the caves without light and showed him how to climb the rocks with his hands.

As time passed, Benny's eyes adjusted to the darkness and he became skilled at maneuvering through the cave system. Mary raised him and communicated with him telepathically. Eventually, Benny grew into a young adult and his curiosity turned towards mating with Mary. She could sense his desires and decided it was time to make him whole by completing his transformation into what she had raised him to be all along. She waited for this day patiently, knowing that their bond would now be even stronger.

She leaned in close and pressed her lips against his, caressing his face with her hands. Benny was taken aback at first, but soon he was eagerly kissing her back. She guided his hand down to her body, showing him what she wanted. He followed her lead, unsure of himself but eager to please.

He hungrily suckled on her breasts as she guided him down towards her waist. She positioned herself above him and he entered her, their bodies moving together in a frenzy. As they reached the peak of pleasure, she bit into his neck and injected her venom. Benny couldn't resist the intense sensations coursing through his body, until suddenly it became too much to bear.

He screamed out in pain as the venom took over his body, transforming him into her loyal servant. She watched with satisfaction as he writhed in agony, unable to speak or communicate with her. His transformation complete, she shut off his mind and claimed him as her own. He tried to speak, but his paralyzed muscles wouldn't allow it.

He was gripped by fear, his breathing quick and heavy as he looked around frantically, not understanding what was happening to him. She reached out and laid her hand on his trembling form, assuring him that everything would be alright.

"This will pass soon, and you will be reborn into a new body."

His body began to change, elongating at the torso while his hips shrank in size. His fingers stretched and sharp claws emerged from their tips, splattering blood onto her as they tore through his flesh. He finally let out a scream, his voice changing along with his physical transformation. He managed to get onto his knees, hunching over as she watched hair sprout from his skin and his spine enlarge and protrude from his back.

She circled around him as he stood up, now with coal-red eyes and black stripes running down the backs of his legs and arms. The stripes were speckled with tiny black dots that blended into his grayish-white skin.

"It's done. You are now my slave, and you will obey me." He looked up at her, still trying to process everything.

"I carry your seed within me, and we will create an offspring together, using your human sperm and my succubus powers. You are now an incubus, forever trapped in your true form. You can only surface at night when I allow it; during the day, you must remain underground. And beware, humans can kill you if they discover your true nature."

His mind was still part human, understanding her words but struggling to comprehend why she had done this to him. With a screech reminiscent of a bat's cry, he darted off into the darkness of the cave.

# 35

## "HOME SWEET HOME"

AFTER DRIVING for 10 long hours, Kai finally arrives at her apartment. Exhausted and drained, she decides to leave her luggage in the car until tomorrow. She stumbles into her bedroom and collapses onto the bed, too tired to even change out of her clothes.

Quickly succumbing to sleep, she awakens abruptly with a sick feeling in her stomach. She sits on the edge of the bed for a few minutes before rushing to the bathroom and vomiting into the toilet. Rinsing her mouth and hands, she stares at herself in the mirror, thinking about Lily's warning if she were to leave.

Lying back in bed and staring up at the ceiling, she murmurs, "Oh Lily, please don't let this be some kind of curse. This is not funny at all."

Rolling over to her side and clutching a pillow tightly, she thinks about Victor as she drifts off to sleep once again.

In her deep slumber, Kai dreams of being with Victor in an open field filled with vibrant flowers as the sun rises. It's not Beaver Creek - it's somewhere else equally beautiful. Suddenly, two young children appear and start playing chase around them. Kai shifts into her fox form and joins in on their game while Victor watches with a smile. The children eventually run up to him and grab his hands while Kai follows behind, still in her shifted form.

As they walk through the field, the child stops and points to a group of four people standing on a ledge, asking their father who they are. Kai immediately senses their presence and becomes defensive. Victor, notices her reaction and stops her from rushing towards them. He knows she can transform into a bear when provoked.

Later that night, Kai wakes up in a panic from a nightmare. She hears her phone beep and realizes it was just a dream. But then, she sees a text from Victor urgently asking to talk to her. She wonders if he somehow knows about her dream or if there is another reason for his late-night message.

Feeling nauseous, she lies back down in bed and feels a hard bulge on her belly. Trying to dismiss it as just a bad dream, she eventually falls back asleep but is woken up again by another text message from Victor. This time, she rushes to the bathroom to vomits again before checking her phone again.

"Please, just call me," Victor begs.

He always seems to know when something is wrong with her. She avoids calling him back, not wanting to break down and cry on the phone. She believes she may be pregnant, and that its Victor's child.

She sobs and lays back on the bed, dreaming of how nice it would be to be a mother. But then she remembers what she saw in the cave and thinks about her own DNA - if she is pregnant, the baby will not be normal. It will be some kind of monster. She cries harder as she feels something pushing against her hand, noticing that her stomach has grown larger.

'No! This can't be happening to me! What am I going to do? I can't have this...this monster growing inside of me.'

Her phone buzzes again with another text from Victor. Frustrated, she finally decides to call him back.

"What do you want?" she snaps.

"Whoa, hold on! What's wrong, Kai? Are you okay?"

"No, I'm not okay, Victor..." she breaks down into tears.

He tries to calm her down so they can talk. She debates whether or not to tell him about what's happening to her.

Finally, he reveals that he had a dream that she was sick and needed him, prompting him to call her immediately. She gives in and confesses everything - how she woke up vomiting a few hours ago, felt a small hard bump in her stomach, and even felt something push against her hand when rubbing her belly.

She tells him she's scared and convinced that she's pregnant with some sort of monster.

"It's not a monster, Kai. It's our child," Victor says soothingly. She breaks down into tears again.

"Please, Kai. Don't do anything to harm yourself or the baby. When we were in the cave together, I felt it - the heat inside you growing. And when my mother threw you, I rushed over and felt the baby. It was cold, and I thought something had happened to it because of her. I almost killed her for hurting you and our child."

"I can't keep it, Victor. We both know the child will inherit my powers and who knows what else. You're a Djinn and a Warlock, you've been alive for centuries and still look like you're in your thirties. Our child would have an impossible life with such a lineage. What if something else impregnated me while we were trapped in that cave?"

Kai's voice begins to rise as she becomes more hysterical.

"Or what if I was violated in the hospital when I was in a coma and no one was there to protect me?"

Victor tries to calm her down.

"But I was there, Kai. Every night. As a Djinn, I have the power to shift to another location and remain invisible unless I choose otherwise."

Kai continues, "That's exactly what I mean by this being a cursed existence. I can't believe this is happening right now. I'm going to see a doctor tomorrow morning and take care of it."

But Victor pleads with her, "Please wait, Kai. I'll leave right now and be there in six hours. I can come to you in spirit form, but I want to be physically present when we handle this together."

Desperate to convince her, he shares his plan, "I'll take you to North Carolina to see a doctor who specializes in cases like ours. He's a Cherokee medicine man who understands our unique genetics and has a clinic at his house for people like us. Your parents probably know of him too."

Kai eventually agrees after much persuasion from Victor and hangs up the phone before curling up with her pillow and drifting off to sleep.

# 36

## "TWINS"

Kai dozes off while waiting for Victor, and soon finds herself deep in slumber. In her dream, she takes on the role of a fierce warrior chasing a Wendi-go through the dense forest. Her spirit animals follow closely behind her as she pursues the elusive creature, flitting through the trees like supernatural beings. Suddenly, a thick fog descends upon them, obscuring her vision and making it difficult to continue the chase. Kai trudges forward, pushing through the waist-high mist that seems to swallow her whole. Frustrated and annoyed, she turns to one of her spirit animals for help, but they just laugh and fly away. She struggles to navigate through the fog, she hears a strange swishing noise and watches as the fog in front of her starts moving away in a wave-like motion. Perplexed and slightly frightened, she can't help but wonder what this mysterious phenomenon could be.

She turns and rushes behind an old tree, she waits motionless as a wave-like movement passes by without noticing her. As it disappears, she cautiously steps out from behind the tree only to have something grab onto her legs and coil around them. She struggles to break free, but the grip only tightens and moves further up her body.

With a sudden jerk, her legs are pulled out from under her, and she falls onto the ground in a thick fog. Something slimy and elongated like a serpent starts crawling up her left leg and enters inside her. She screams in agony as it penetrates deeper into her body. Desperately trying to clear the fog and see what is happening, she realizes that it is a black serpent-like creature. She frantically reaches down between her legs to remove it, but its slippery and powerful hold makes it impossible for her to grasp. Suddenly, two arms emerge from either side of the serpent and grab onto hers, pulling her back down onto the ground.

"No, you can't take my baby! No, you can't!" she screams out in terror. Then, she hears someone calling her name.

"Kai, Kai, wake up. It's just a dream." She flails her arms around trying to hit whoever is above her. Feeling someone grabbing her arms, she lets out another piercing scream.

"Kai, calm down...it's me, Victor."

As she finally recognizes her attacker, she stops screaming and hitting him.

"Victor, they wanted to take my baby! They tried to steal it from me."

"Who did, Kai?"

"I don't know. Some serpent-like creature pulled me down and violated me, trying to rip the baby out of my womb."

"It was just a nightmare...it wasn't real. You're safe now, I'm here with you."

He holds her in his lap as she clings onto him for comfort. He asks if he can feel the baby, and she guides his hand to her belly. He feels a bump and then another one, causing him to laugh with surprise. But then he starts feeling a warm tingling sensation.

"Wow, that's something new!" he exclaims.

"What do you mean, new?" she retorts angrily.

"Calm down, I meant it in a good way. I've never felt anything like that before."

He touches her belly again and this time he feels two distinct heads.

"What is this?" he mutters in confusion.

She suddenly jumps up from his lap.

"What is it, Victor? What did you feel? Is it some kind of monster?" she accuses, glaring at him as if ready to attack him.

"No, it's not a monster."

"Then what is it, Prince Charming?" she spits out sarcastically.

"Now Kai, just relax. Your hormones are probably just elevated and..."

"You think so, Mr. Perfect?" she interrupts bitterly.

"Kai...please calm down and sit back on my lap. Let me hold you and make you feel safe."

"No. Tell me what the hell you felt," she demands.

"Fine. I felt two heads inside of you."

Kai's eyes widened as she processed the news. "So I'm carrying twin monsters or a two-headed dragon? That's just great, Victor!" She exclaimed.

"Do you have any tea?" Victor replied calmly.

"Tea?... Of course, I have tea!" Kai said, clearly agitated.

"I'll make us some hot tea and then we can go see the medicine man," Victor suggested.

"So, he can remove this two-headed beast from me?" Kai retorted sarcastically.

"Whatever you want to do, Kai," Victor responded, getting up from his chair and heading into the kitchen to prepare the tea. As he waited for the water to boil, he mentally prepared himself for what was to come - telling Kai that her babies would grow faster than normal human babies. He knew she would be furious.

Returning to the living room with a cup of chamomile tea, he found Kai pacing back and forth in a state of panic.

"Kai, please come sit down and join me for some hot tea," Victor urged, placing the cup on the table for her.

But when she looked at him with one blue eye and one green eye, he knew things were serious. Her body was in defense mode and forcing a shift could harm the babies inside her.

"Please, Kai, sit down," Victor pleaded, taking her hand, and leading her to the couch. She reluctantly sat down and began drinking her tea.

After finishing her cup, Kai had calmed down significantly. She leaned back on the couch and scooted closer to Victor, resting her head in his lap as she curled up. Victor gently stroked her hair and face, looking down at her belly where they both felt two distinct bumps beneath their hands. Tears welled up in

Victor's eyes as he realized the gravity of their situation and held back from expressing his emotions so as not to upset Kai.

"We need to take you to the medicine man, Kai."

"I know, Victor. But for now, let's just enjoy this moment together." She stands up and leads him into the bedroom, where she shows him the shower. He can get ready while she packs some clothes. He grabs her hand and pulls her into the bathroom with him.

Taking off her clothes slowly, he twirls her around and presses her against his chest. Holding her tightly, he kisses her neck while caressing her breasts and belly. They step into the shower.

The water running over them kissing Victor slowly turns her around and she bends holding onto the shower handle she feels him spread her legs so he can put himself inside her.

"Are you sure this won't hurt me? Or the monsters try coming out during our sex?"

"Shhh, hush just enjoy this honey I promise it won't hurt at all." Victor says as he slowly pushes himself inside her.

The moan coming from Kai assures him that she is enjoying this. He slides himself back and thrusts a little harder into her. With every move he makes the more she moans in pleasure. Grabbing her hips Victor thrusts deeper. Kai screams in pleasure asking for more and faster. Soon she is begging for him to cum inside her.

"Oh, Victor that was amazing." Kai says as she turns around and kisses him.

"You're amazing my little fox."

They both exit the shower and dry off.

"I'm starving how about you Kai?"

"Yes so am I. My appetite finally came back. So tired of throwing up."

"Lets cook breakfast and then I need to call my boss." Kai says.

"I have work tomorrow morning."

She calls his cell phone but gets no answer. So, she leaves a message for him to call back when he gets the chance. Then she calls her mother and asks where she went when she was pregnant with Kai. Her mother tells her they went to the medicine man's house.

"Why are you asking me this, Kai?"

"I never knew. I thought you went to the hospital like everyone else."

"Oh no, Kai, my DNA was different. I couldn't risk having humans outside of our tribe testing my blood. If you ever get pregnant, make sure you call me so I can tell you who to see."

"Well, Mom, I am pregnant now. Who should I see?"

"Kai, stop joking around. This is serious business."

"I'm not joking, 'Grandma.'"

"Kai, you're pregnant? When did you find out? I need to know; it's important."

"I just found out about a day ago. Why? Is something wrong?"

"You need to find a medicine man right away. Don't waste any time, Kai. You need to go now. The baby needs a medicine man to slow down its growth or it will grow faster than your body can handle. You could lose the baby. It's very painful if you don't seek a medicine man."

"I'm going to one in North Carolina...a Cherokee medicine man."

"You're going to Jacy Redbone?"

"Let me ask, hold on. Victor, who is the medicine man you're taking me to?"

"Nosh Whiteriver and Jacy Redbone. They work together as a team."

"Yes, Jacy Redbone and his partner Nosh Whiteriver."

"Nosh Whiteriver is very good but Jacy Redbone is the best. You're in good hands with them, Kai. Trust what they tell you and do what they say. Take whatever they give you. They have powers that no one else has, and your baby will be perfect."

"I think it might be twins, Mom."

"Twins, Kai?" Kai's mother exclaimed with astonishment.

"This is a sign. According to legend, twins can bring great power- but it all depends on their genders." She continued, explaining the different outcomes if Kai had twin boys, girls, or one of each.

"Whatever the case may be, these twins will play a crucial role in fighting against the evil forces that threaten our shape-shifting community."

Kai nodded, recalling her previous conversation with Lily about the power inside her that she needed to discover. Her mother confirmed that Lily was right and asked who the father of the twins was.

Kai hesitated before answering truthfully, "His name is Victor...and he is a Djinn and a warlock."

"Oh, my dear, Kai. So, you're a silver blood shifter and he's a powerful being. These babies are going to be even stronger than we could have ever imagined."

Feeling relieved and excited, Kai hung up the phone and told Victor about her conversation with her mom.

"We need to pack you a few things and leave Kai, we are on limited time."

"But I need to tell my boss I'm not coming in." Kai replies.

"Well call him on the way to North Carolina, we have to go and we need to get there tonight at the latest. I've called and told Dr. Redbone about this while you were on the phone with your mom. He's already getting things prepared for our arrival."

As they continued their journey towards Dr. Redbone's property, Kai couldn't help but wonder how she would balance raising two powerful children with her current job.

"You'll have to quit your job and move in with me," Victor said matter-of-factly. "We'll raise these babies together and protect them from any harm."

As they approached the gates of Dr. Redbone's property, they were greeted by a voice through a speaker. Kai notices all the cameras mounted around the area. A large man appeared from the shadows as they drove through the gates, startling both Kai and Victor.

"It must be one of the guards on the property." Victor remarks.

"Why would they need guards?" Kai questions. "He moved too quickly to just be a guard."

"That's because he's a special kind of guard, Kai. He's a shape shifter he looked like a wolf."

As they pass by more guards, Kai can't help but stare at how tall, and the muscular frame, dressed in all black with open shirt that shows off their ripped arms, muscular abs and black fur. One guard catches Kai's eye. His face is mostly hidden in shadow, but his piercing blue eyes are visible. He watches her pass in the car.

Kai is fascinated by this creature, admiring his strength and beauty. The guard nods at them. Victor catches a glimpse of him in the rearview mirror before he disappears into the darkness with incredible speed.

They arrive at a large house attached to a big clinic, where two men are standing outside. One has long white hair in braids with a feather at the back, giving off a wise and ancient vibe. The other man is tall and thin with straight black hair and reddish tan skin, appearing to be in his late forties. Victor introduces them as Jacy Redbone and Nosh Whiteriver - both special shape shifters and healers who have been waiting for Kai's arrival.

"Hello, Victor. Nice to see you again; you're looking well my son," Jacy greets them.

"What do you mean 'son'?" Kai asks in confusion.

"Oh, did I not mention? This is my father, Dr. Jacy Redbone." Victor explains.

Kai can hardly believe what she's hearing as she walks towards the doors with disbelief written all over her face.

"Victor you have a lot of explaining to do." Kai says.

"Hello Kai, we are so glad to meet you. Let's get you in the chair and to the ceremony room." Dr. Redbone says.

"Nice to meet you sir, and I can walk just fine."

"Kai, just get in the chair. It's a clinic they wheel you in, just let them do their job honey." Victor says.

Kai nods in agreement.

"But why a ceremonial room." Kai ask confused.

*To Be Continued.........*

# PLACES AND PEOPLE
# INFLUENCED THE STORY

Places and People used to create the story:

John Smith is a character based off my Father in Law John Eaton Sr.

Lizzie Smith is a character based off my Mother in law Louise Eaton

Kyle is a character based off my husband Kyle Eaton

Hurley is a character that is really Hurley a dog that is my in laws.

Beaver Creek is a real place in Kentucky where my in laws live.

The property is real sets in the town of Monticello Kentucky.

And sulfur Mountain is actually the mountain that is near the property

Some of the tales are true from neighbors that live near my in laws.

The rest is fiction..

# CONTACT THE AUTHOR

authorbellafrost@gmail.com

facebook.com/BellaFrostAuthor

amazon.com/stores/Bella-Frost/author/B08D8MSJXP